"I feel like such a fool," I said. "The way I behaved to you before, and then crying tonight. . . ."

"Don't you cry much?" Bruce asked, wiping a tear from my cheek with his fingertip.

"I sort of got out of the habit," I said, realizing that I hadn't really cried since the divorce. I had simply shut off my feelings—until tonight.

"Well," he said, "crying's a good thing to do when you're sad." He smiled and gave me a wonderful hug. "You know, I thought you were one of these stuck up sort of girls who only cares about herself. I never thought I'd see you crying for koala bears."

"I think I had myself all wrong, too," I said quietly. "And I'm so sorry about—"

"No!" Bruce said firmly, putting a finger on my lips. "No more apologizing. Everything that happened before tonight is forgotten, understood?"

I even managed to smile. "Understood," I said.

Lovebirds

Janet Quin-Harkin

BANTAM BOOKS
TORONTO • NEW YORK • LONDON • SYDNEY • AUCKLAND

RL 6, IL age 11 and up

LOVEBIRDS
A Bantam Book / August 1984

Cover photo by Pat Hill

ISBN 0-553-24181-8

*Published simultaneously in the United States
and Canada*

PRINTED IN THE UNITED STATES OF AMERICA

O   0 9 8 7 6 5 4 3 2 1

Chapter One

Have you ever had a day that starts out perfectly and ends up a complete disaster? I didn't know I was having one of those days as I walked home from school that brisk November afternoon, humming happily under my breath. I didn't know the best day of my life was about to be ruined and that my life was about to undergo a complete change.

I'd woken up that Monday morning to a gorgeous winter day. The sun was glinting off the snow-covered trees, and the air smelled fresh and clean. I had stretched happily, taken a long, luxurious shower, and washed my ginger brown hair. I had put on my favorite skirt, burgundy wool with threads of black and red woven into it, and spent some time working on my makeup. I want to be a fashion model, and so I always take the time to do my face perfectly.

One thing I've never been able to do with makeup is cover the sprinkling of freckles on my nose. They're so annoying. But a little eyeliner makes my blue eyes bright and big.

That morning I had looked at myself in the full-length mirror on my closet door. "Pretty hot, Tiffany Johns," I said to my reflection. My new boots looked great with my outfit, and they gave me the extra height I needed. I'm only five feet six inches, and I need to grow at least another inch if I'm ever going to make it as a model.

I had downed a glass of orange juice and set out for school a little early. It was so nice out, I decided to walk the long way. Good thing, too, because halfway down Butterfield Lane I heard a car honk beside me. It was Greg Sanders in his red English sports car, and he wanted to give me a lift!

What you've got to know about Greg is that he's the most popular guy at school. His black hair flops across his forehead in the cutest way, and his dark eyes absolutely sparkle. He'd been dating Janelle Patterson for years until they broke up a few weeks before. Everyone was wondering who he'd ask out next.

I knew Greg because we had been lab partners in biology. We'd cut up worms together —or rather, Greg had done most of the cutting, and we'd giggled when Mr. Rosenberg wasn't looking. Greg had made biology bearable, and ever since then, I had really liked him a lot. Of course, I didn't think I'd be the lucky one he'd ask out. I mean, I'm definitely popular, but I'm not a leader. I figured he'd ask Marcia Laird. She was always in the center of things, planning pep rallies and dances and stuff.

So I was absolutely amazed when I got into Greg's car and he said, "Tiffany, I'm glad I caught up with you. I was wondering if you've already got a date for the winter formal."

I couldn't believe Greg was asking me to the dance. I tried to think of a sophisticated answer. "Well, if you're inviting, I'm accepting," I said with a winning smile.

"Great," Greg said. "Shall we seal it with a kiss?" He leaned over slowly, took my chin in his hand, and gave me a gentle kiss. I couldn't have thought of a better way to start the day.

I walked around all morning with a silly grin on my face. I didn't even feel like telling anyone that I was the lucky one Greg had asked. I wanted to enjoy my secret alone for the day and tell the others later. I didn't think things could be any better—until lunch when

Marcia asked me to be in charge of makeup for the talent show. I'd taken a makeup course and experimented with it a lot because of my interest in modeling, and I was glad Marcia liked what I did with it. It was really an honor to be asked. Only the most popular kids worked on the talent show.

I walked home that day, hoping I could persuade my mother to buy me a new dress for the dance and dreaming up new makeup approaches for the show. *How lucky can you get?* I asked myself. *Just two years ago you were petrified moving from California to New York after the divorce. Now, you've not only survived a new high school on the other side of the country, but you've become part of the top crowd and gotten Greg Sanders to ask you to the dance.* What more could a girl want—except perhaps a modeling contract!

Walking down our normally sedate Main Street, I noticed that several stores already had Christmas displays in their windows, and this was Thanksgiving week.

Seeing the windows made me wonder what the holidays at our house would be like that year. My mother was not exactly the celebrating type. She liked things neat, and Christmas was messy with ribbons and bits of wrapping paper on the carpets. I couldn't remember the last time Mom had fussed in the kitchen; we would probably go to a restaurant for both Thanksgiving and Christmas again. My mother would buy me another expensive outfit for Christmas. Her boyfriend Felix would probably bring me something dumb like a big doll. Felix didn't understand much about teenagers.

I pushed those unpleasant thoughts out of my mind. *I can't wait to tell Mom about Greg,* I thought, trying to recapture my rosy glow again. *I hope she's home from work early so that we can have a cozy dinner and celebrate.* But as I opened the front door, I heard the sound of voices from the living room.

"Is that you, Tiffany, darling?" my mother called. "Do come in here, I have a lovely surprise for you."

I pushed open the living room door and found my mother sitting on the white sofa in a purple pajama suit. She looked up and smiled as I came in. "Look, dear, Felix is here," she cooed to me.

Felix was perched on the edge of a leather and chrome chair. He was wearing a dreadful baby blue turtleneck, and his bald spot was showing through his hair, which he'd tried to hide by combing his hair forward. *Is this supposed to be "a lovely surprise," finding Felix here?* I thought gloomily.

"And how's my future fashion queen?" Felix asked heartily. "You certainly are getting tall fast. You've grown at least an inch since the last time I saw you."

"You saw me four days ago," I said. "If I'm growing at that rate, you'd better sign me up for a pro basketball team." Felix smiled, but my mother didn't look as if she thought the joke were funny. "Anyway, I thought you were going on a cruise," I said to Felix.

"I couldn't stay away from your adorable mother," he said, smoothing down his sparse hair from back to front.

"Felix decided not to take that particular cruise," my mother said. "He decided it wouldn't be any fun all alone. So he came over today, and he—" She looked across to Felix.

"I've asked your mother to marry me," Felix said.

I looked from one to the other, trying to digest this piece of information. It was about as easy to take as if someone had told me space invaders were crawling down the Empire State Building. "Felix wants to marry you?" I asked, my voice barely audible.

"That's right, darling," my mother cooed.

"And I've accepted. We're going to be married a week from Saturday, and then we'll be going on a long Pacific Ocean cruise. Isn't that wonderful news?"

"Oh, sure," I said, gulping back an annoying lump that was creeping into my throat. "Best news I've had all day!"

Then I ran to my room and locked the door.

I didn't cry. I had cried very little since the divorce. I think I cried so much then, I didn't have any tears left. Instead, I walked to my dressing table, sat down. "My mother marrying Felix?" I asked the person in the mirror. "Can that possibly be true?"

My reflection stared back with a hopeless expression. I slid my hands over the cool glass surface of the table. It was not the sort of dressing table I had wanted, it was all chrome and glass like most of my mother's furniture. I had asked for an old-fashioned one, one made of polished oak, but my mother had refused. "We have to coordinate, darling," she had said. "We just don't have a folksy sort of house." But that day I was glad for that glass. It was cold and impersonal, and somehow it felt soothing to slide my fingers over it, back and forth, back and forth.

There was a gentle tap on my door. "Tiffy,

honey, may I come in?" my mother pleaded. "Tiffy, open the door, baby, and let's talk." With a sigh I got up and walked slowly across the room, dragging my feet through the thick nylon carpet.

"Tiffany, let me come in so we can talk this thing over," my mother said as soon as I opened the door.

"There's nothing to talk over," I replied. "You've decided to marry Felix. That's all there is to it."

"But I want you to be happy, too, baby. I want what's best for both of us. Why don't we sit and talk about it?"

"Do you want me in on this discussion?" came Felix's voice from the living room.

"No, thank you, darling," she called. "This is girl talk. Why don't you fix yourself a martini, and we'll join you in a moment." Then she followed me into my room and shut the door again. "I just can't understand why you're so upset," she said, looking at me with big, bewildered eyes. "I thought you liked Felix!"

"I don't dislike him," I said. "But that doesn't mean I want him as a father."

"But surely you saw it coming," my mother pleaded, throwing herself across my white bedspread. "You must have seen how I felt about Felix."

I shook my head bleakly and sat down at my dressing table again. "I thought he was just a boyfriend."

"I can't understand your hostility," my mother said. "Felix is a wonderful person. He's warm and gentle and considerate. He likes to be surrounded by order and beautiful things, unlike your father, who seems to enjoy traipsing around in the mud. Felix and I are so perfect for each other. I had been hoping and hoping that he would ask me to marry him, and now I'm overjoyed. The only thing spoiling my happiness is that you aren't happy, too."

That made me feel pretty guilty. I got up and walked over to her. "I do want you to be happy, Mom," I said, "but I just hadn't expected this. I suppose I could do worse than have Felix Grant for a stepfather." Then a thought struck me. "You will still want me around when you get married, won't you?"

My mother put her arms around me, hugging me fiercely. "Of course we will, darling. Felix just adores you."

"Well, that's a relief," I said. "I thought you might be moving to his apartment in Manhattan and that there wouldn't be room for me, too."

"Of course not, baby," she said. "We *are* thinking about living in the city because Felix just wouldn't be happy in the suburbs. But we'll find an apartment that's just right for all of us. So don't worry about it. We're not even going to start looking for a new place until we come back from the cruise."

Thoughts of facing a new high school flashed through my mind. I hastily pushed them aside. I had enough problems to cope with right then! "By the way," I asked, "what's going to happen to me while you're on this cruise?"

"That's all taken care of, darling," she said. "Your father has been bugging me about seeing you more often. Now he's going to get his chance. I phoned him and told him to expect you a week from Sunday."

"I can't go then!" I blurted out. "That's way before Christmas vacation."

"I know, darling, but it couldn't be helped," my mother said soothingly. "The ship we want to sail on leaves that afternoon, and we've had to plan everything around that. I thought it wouldn't matter if you took off those extra weeks from school. You could catch up, and you wouldn't miss much, would you?"

"Oh, no," I said, finding that I was about to cry after all. "Only the biggest dance of the year with the most popular guy at school. Mom, Greg Sanders asked me to go. There's no way I can miss that dance."

"Oh, honey," Mom said easily. "You said Greg was just a friend from class, not a boyfriend."

"He wasn't—before."

"What I meant was, I never got the idea that you felt passionately about him."

"Mom," I said, annoyed, "all the girls want to go out with Greg. He chose me over everyone else."

"Tiffany, I guess I just don't understand. If you really liked the boy, I could see why you'd be upset. But if this is just a matter of status, how can you care more about one date with him than an extended visit with your father and brother?"

You're right, Mom, you don't understand, I thought bitterly.

"Anyway," my mother continued, "I haven't told you the best part. Your father is making another one of his movies, and he wants to take you along. And you'll never guess where they're filming. Australia!"

For a moment my stomach flip-flopped with excitement. Maybe there would be a part for me, something that could help me with my modeling career. But, no. Dad's movies weren't glamorous. He was a real outdoors type, and his films were either documentaries or docu-dramas about wildlife and hiking nuts. Oh, well, if there weren't a part for me, maybe I could help with the makeup. All actors used makeup, didn't they? And Australia did sound pretty interesting. It might just be fun.

Chapter Two

The next morning my gang was waiting at school, as they usually did, at the bottom of the main staircase.

"What's this we hear?" Marcia called as soon as she saw me coming down the hall. "There's a rumor going around that Greg Sanders has asked you to the winter formal."

"What luck," Elizabeth said. "Do you know how many girls have been chasing him all year—me included. How did you manage it?"

"Oh, just her charm, her wit, and her dazzling good looks," Becky cut in. They all laughed.

"Well, is it true or isn't it?" Marcia asked. "We ought to know if something unusual is happening. And Greg Sanders is definitely unusual."

"Yes, he asked me," I said, trying to stop my voice from breaking, "and that's the good news. The bad news is I can't go."

"Why not?" Elizabeth shrieked.

"If your mother won't let you, tell her we will all picket your house until she gives in," Becky cried.

"If you have a term paper, we'll write it for you," Elizabeth chimed in.

I had to smile in spite of my misery. "Believe me," I said. "I wouldn't miss the dance for any of those things. Unfortunately the reason happens to be a bit bigger than that. My mother is getting married again."

"No!" "For real?" "Who to?" they all asked at once.

"Felix," I said and sighed.

"Not Felix the creep?" Becky asked in horror. She had met him several times; so she could speak from experience.

"The very same."

"How terrible—poor you," Janet said. "Do you think he'll wear a turtleneck with his tux to the wedding?"

"Maybe he'll get a really great band to play at the reception—like the Lawrence Welk Orchestra," Marcia added, giggling.

"Maybe he'll get a toupee instead of combing his stringy hair forward," Elizabeth continued.

"It's all very well for you to laugh," I said. "You haven't got to spend the rest of your life under the same roof with a guy who thinks the Police write parking tickets and a late night out is ten-thirty."

"We really do sympathize," Elizabeth said. "We only laughed because he's so funny, in a revolting sort of way."

"What I don't understand," Becky said, "is why your mother's wedding is going to stop you from going to a dance. After all, if she's getting her romance, why can't you?"

"A small matter of a honeymoon," I replied. "Their ship sails five days before the dance. I'm getting shipped off to my father so that my mother won't have to feel guilty about me."

"But you could stay with me that week," Becky said. "My dad would drive you to the airport. I know he would."

I sighed. "You know how stubborn my mother gets. For some reason she's determined that I be safely delivered to my father before she goes off into the sunset with Felix."

"I never even knew your father was alive," Elizabeth said. "You don't talk about him."

"I know. My parents didn't part on the best of terms, and I haven't seen my dad in over two years."

"Didn't he get visitation rights or anything?" Janet asked.

"Sure, but my mother is always very clever about making arrangements that just don't work out."

"Boy, that's mean—if you like your father, that is," Marcia said. "Personally I'd be only too glad to have an excuse not to see much of mine. Whenever he does take me out, all he does is quiz me about schoolwork—how am I doing in math? Have I started studying for the SATs? What a bore."

"Oh, I like my father a lot," I said. "In fact, I'd be really happy to go to California and see him if I didn't have to miss the dance with Greg."

"He lives in California?" Julie asked excitedly. She wanted to be a TV star.

"That's right. In Beverly Hills, actually. And I'll be going with him to Australia to make a movie," I added smugly.

"Beverly Hills! And he's making a movie! Is he an actor?"

"He's a director, but not like Steven Spielberg or one of those people. He's an outdoor type, who makes docudramas and documentaries. You know, people setting balloon records or rafting down rapids."

"He doesn't sound at all like your mother,"

Becky said. "In fact, he sounds like a direct opposite."

"You're right, he is. The most athletic thing my mother does is file her nails. The one time my father took her camping, a bug got into her sleeping bag, and she screamed so loudly that the forest ranger thought a bear was after her."

"So why did they get married in the first place?" Janet asked.

I shrugged my shoulders. "Beats me. They were both working in movies. My mother was a costume designer, and my father was the camera person for the same picture. They were young, and I suppose my mother was very beautiful—"

"Yeah, people do some crazy things when they're in love," Elizabeth agreed. "By the way, when are you going to tell Greg that you can't go to the dance with him?"

"I guess it'll have to wait until after school."

"We could spread your story around," Marcia said thoughtfully. "That way, the news would be broken to him gently."

"No," I said. "I think I'd rather tell him myself. Things tend to get twisted by third persons. He might think I don't want to go with him."

"So, what's this movie you'll be working on?" Marcia asked.

"Actually, I'm not sure," I answered, not telling them that I might not even be working on the film. "I'm hoping there'll be some cute actors who like to go out dancing. But I'll tell you all about it when I get back."

"Oh, definitely," Becky said. "Well, good luck. How long will you be gone?"

"Till after the Christmas vacation—almost five weeks. One in California and the rest in Australia."

"Five weeks! You'd better be back in time to plan the talent show," Marcia said, "or I'll have to get someone to take your place on the committee."

That was another thing I hadn't thought of—losing my job as makeup artist. Right then it seemed as though life were out to get me!

My little talk with Greg went OK. He said it was terrible that I had to miss the dance and made jokes about me forgetting him and dating some blond surfer in California. It was hard to tell if he was hurt or mad. We all had a habit of making jokes out of things rather than saying what we really felt. We all pretended that life was one big laugh and we'd be fine as long as we kept on smiling. Suddenly I wondered if Greg *really* cared about me at all. In a way, Mom had been right when she'd said our relationship was friendly rather than passionate. What had she called our date? A matter of status.

With the Thanksgiving holiday and having to shop for a dress for the wedding, the time flew by. Becky came by to help me pack after school the Friday before the wedding.

"You're taking all this stuff?" she asked. "You look like you're going away for a year."

"I have to show them how sophisticated we are on the East Coast," I said. "And besides, my father still thinks of me as a little girl. I want him to see how much I've matured. But he probably won't even notice," I added, remembering how unobservant he was. "He never used to notice what my mother wore, which was one of the things that bugged her most. She likes to be noticed."

"What's she going to wear for the wedding?" Becky asked, cramming a pile of clothes into one of my suitcases. "Are she and Felix going to color coordinate?"

"I don't know about him," I said, "but she's wearing this gorgeous peach-colored silk with a really low-cut back."

19

"And what about you, didn't you get a new dress, too?"

"Yeah, but for the first time in years, I'm not excited about a new dress. In fact, nothing about this wedding excites me."

"You know, these clothes won't be suitable for shooting rapids and sky diving," Becky said. She picked up my favorite red mini-dress that buttoned down the side and had padded shoulders. "You said that's the kind of stuff your father is into."

I looked up and frowned. "I don't intend to do anything more athletic or dangerous than sit by a pool and lift a cool drink to my lips," I said. "When it comes to roughing it, I take strictly after my mother. My father and brother can go and do their rough stuff and leave me at home."

"You have a brother?" Becky said excitedly. "How old? What's his name?"

"Eighteen, and his name is Adam."

"Wow, an eighteen-year-old brother, and you keep quiet about him! What sort of friend are you?"

"You wouldn't like him," I said. "He's into bugs, and he keeps jars of creepy things in his room."

"He might have improved with age," Becky said. "If he's grown up cute, don't forget to ask him if he wants a sophisticated New York pen pal."

"I only hope his friends don't all like bugs, too," I said. "I'm looking forward to a few wild parties. You know how strict my mother is about staying out late. I intend to make the most of my time away from her."

"Boy, you're so lucky," Becky said. "I can just picture all those pool parties at fancy houses in Beverly Hills, and Australia sounds exotic. Bet actors really know how to have a good time."

"Don't worry, Beck, I'll send you a postcard describing it all," I said, laughing.

"Just pack up a few cute, suntanned Californians or Australians and bring them back for us," Becky said. "Hey, is it six o'clock already? My mother will kill me if I don't get home in time for dinner. I've got to go. Bye, Tiffany. See you when you get back!"

Then she was gone. I realized afterward that she, like Greg, hadn't said she would miss me. No one else had, either. But then, I hadn't told them I would miss them. That was just how things were with my friends. We joked and laughed a lot, but we never really got close to one another. I suppose I had deliberately chosen to be with a group of kids who cared most about clothes and rock music and very little about anything not superficial. I guess I hadn't wanted to get close to anyone. After the divorce I had definitely made a point of staying away from anything or anyone emotional.

The wedding, which was held at a hotel, went off very smoothly. I couldn't believe how quickly my mother had organized it. She looked stunning in her peach silk. Felix looked uncomfortable in his tux and kept smoothing down his combed-forward hair—just in case his bald spot was showing through. All their friends were elegant and beautifully dressed. The women's perfectly made-up faces looked like china masks. Everyone made a big fuss over me, telling me I looked just like my mother. My crowning moment came when a refined, gray-haired woman asked me if I had ever done any modeling and I found out she was an editor at *Vogue.*

So I was in a very hopeful mood as I headed for California the day after the wedding. Before me, I had almost five weeks of relaxed living, a chance to show off my New York fashions and practically a promise of a modeling career when I got back. *So what if I miss one dance?* I told myself, relaxing into my airplane seat and pretending that I crossed the country alone all the time. *When I come back in January with a terrific tan, Greg will still be there—if I want him, that is,* I added, thinking about what my mother had said. Then I closed my eyes and fell into a very nice daydream in which I appeared on the cover of *Vogue.*

I did have a few moments of panic, just before we landed in L.A., thinking about living with my father. Our last few years together before the divorce had been spoiled by fights and shouting matches. But I knew my father was basically an easygoing guy and that he was looking forward to seeing me again. After all, two years is a long time to be without your only daughter.

He was there just outside the barrier, and his face lit up immediately. "Tiffany," he called, stepping toward me and giving me a big bear hug. "You look beautiful, and you've grown so much."

"I should hope so," I said. "If I hadn't grown since you last saw me, I'd be a midget."

He laughed, and I remembered how I had always liked that deep, rumbling sound. He looked well, really healthy. Good-looking, too, but not dressed up at all. I had gotten my ginger hair and blue eyes from him. Funny, though, I still resembled my mother more. I guess our styles were more the same. I mean, I'm not the big muscular type Dad is.

"How was the wedding?" he asked.

"Elegant. Full of beautiful people all talking about how beautiful they were."

"That should have pleased your mother," he said. "She likes things to be that way."

We got my luggage and walked to where Dad had parked the car. "Tiffany," Dad said, slinging my two suitcases into the trunk of his car, "you sure don't pack lightly. What have you got in these?"

"Just some clothes I need," I said.

"I hope you mean hiking gear," he answered. "I wouldn't want you to have the wrong idea about this movie. We're going to be in rough country. And, by the way, our schedule has been moved up. We'll be leaving in two days." Dad stepped on the gas, and we roared onto the highway toward his house.

"Oh, but I wanted to spend some time on the beaches here and get a good suntan before we go!" I cried. "I look so much better with a tan."

Dad just sighed. We spent the rest of the ride in silence.

I took one step inside my father's house, then stopped in amazement. "Oh, my goodness," I gasped.

My father laughed uneasily. "Yes, it is a bit messy, isn't it? But we're taking a lot of this stuff with us to Australia."

Personally, I thought "a bit messy" could hardly begin to describe what I saw in front of me. My father and brother lived in an elegant apartment building with palm trees in front and a big sparkling pool in the courtyard. The marble lobby of the building was filled with potted ferns. So I was totally unprepared for the disaster area right inside my father's front door. The living room was large and opened right onto the kitchen and dining area. Every inch of space was covered with boxes, bags, yesterday's coffee mugs, empty Coke cans, and an odd boot here or there. I had expected my father and brother to live a bit more primitively than my mother and me, but not like that!

"Daddy, it's terrible!" I said before I could stop myself. "How can you live like this?" And I started rushing around the room gathering all the dirty glasses together and carrying them toward the kitchen. It was a useless thing to do since the kitchen sink was already piled high with dirty dishes.

"Just leave that stuff," my father said sharply. "We don't normally let it get this way, but we had a little farewell party last night, and then we got out all the stuff to pack. We just haven't had time to clean up. Come on through here, I'll show you your room."

He led me across the living room, stepping carefully between the piles of objects, and opened a door, motioning me ahead of him. As I stepped inside, a huge something, white and furry, rose from the bed and launched itself at me.

I took one look, screamed, and ran. It was a good thing my father grabbed my arm, or I might have been at the Mexican border and still running by the time they caught up with me. "Hey, slow down a minute," he said. "It's only Bigfoot."

At that moment I could easily have believed that my father had captured a bigfoot and hidden it in my bedroom, but when I had stopped shaking, I saw that it was only a gigantic white dog, now standing beside me and peering at me as if he thought I was completely bananas. He stepped forward and licked my hand. "Nice doggy," I said in a shaky voice.

"He won't hurt you," my father said, a little annoyed. "He's only trying to make friends."

"But he's so big," I said. "Has he eaten yet

today? I don't like the way he keeps looking at me as if I were a steak."

"Oh, come on, Tiffany," my father said. "You used to like dogs when you were a little girl."

"Yes, well, I haven't had much to do with them for quite a few years," I said. "And the only dog I know in Westchester always makes a grab at my ankle. If your dog did that, I'd lose a whole leg."

My father roughly stroked the dog's fur, and Bigfoot thumped his enormous tail on the floor. I decided I was glad we were going away in two days so that I didn't have to spend a whole week keeping out of the dog's way.

All of a sudden Bigfoot launched himself like a canine rocket again, bringing another scream from me. Only this time the launch was not in my direction. It was down the hall toward the front door, where Adam had just come in.

"Hi, there, old feller," Adam was saying while I could hear two hundred pounds of crazy dog leaping up and down. "Have you got her, Dad?" he called down the hall.

"She's in here with me," my father called back. Adam came running toward us.

"Hey, Tiffany," he said, stopping shyly before he reached me and thinking better of hugging me at the last minute. "Hey, you've grown up. You look like something out of a fashion magazine."

"Thanks," I said. "You've grown up, too." He really had. The thought flashed through my head that Becky wanted me to wrap him up and ship him East if he turned out to be cute. And he certainly was cute. He was big like my father, at least six two, and his muscles showed through the old UCLA T-shirt he was wearing. All the acne I remembered had miraculously cleared up, and his hair was streaked blond from the California sun. *It's too bad he's my brother,* I thought. *I wonder if he's got some equally cute friends.*

"So how's New York?" he asked politely.

"Cold at this time of year."

"And how's your school?"

"Just like any school, I guess—boring."

"And how's Mom?" he asked awkwardly.

"When I last saw her, she was sailing into the sunset wearing a Diane Von Furstenberg dress and a silly grin on her face."

My father frowned, and Adam coughed as if he was embarrassed. "Go bring Tiffany's luggage in for her to unpack, will you, Adam?" my father asked. He turned to me. "You'll have to repack, honey. It seems like you brought a lot of stuff we can't bring to Australia. Forget the special dresses. You won't need them. Just bring your jeans and some T-shirts. We'll have to buy you some hiking gear since I assume you don't have any."

There was a loud exclamation from Adam down the hall. "Hey, look at all this stuff, Dad! It's more than we're bringing combined with camera stuff. Why'd you bring all this, Tiff?"

"Oh," I said, "these are just a few of my clothes. I wasn't quite sure what I would need, and I wanted to play it safe."

"Play it safe!" Adam exclaimed, dumping my two huge suitcases on the bed. "You could open a couple of stores if these are all clothes." He took my coat off his shoulder and started to lay it in the big overstuffed chair.

I let out a yelp of horror. "Don't put it there. That chair's full of dog hairs. I'll never get them off, and they'll show on the dark blue."

Adam looked at me as if I were weird and handed me the coat, which I hung up.

"How about we go out for some Mexican food," Dad said, giving Adam a warning glance. "Tiffany doesn't seem to like the look of our kitchen."

"I don't mind cleaning it up for you, honestly I don't," I said. "You don't have to eat out just for me."

"We eat out a lot, like a few times a week, don't we, Dad?" Adam said. "We're too lazy to cook!"

Adam and Dad exchanged amused glances, and I felt a stab of jealousy. My brother really knew my father while I barely did. We seemed so far apart, Dad and I. My father took me by the arm, and we walked outside. The warm breeze felt wonderful to me after the biting cold of New York. Dad was looking at me hard and frowning. "You know, Tiffany," he said, "you've really changed. You used to be spunky and daring. Now you're turning into a small version of your mother."

"I am not!" I said angrily. "I don't like the way she and her friends act at all. They're so—so artificial. All they care about is how beautiful they look and how many people notice them. They're so status conscious."

"I'm sorry," my father said, "I guess I misjudged. But you'd only been in my house one minute when you started tidying it up. You were terrified of my dog. You brought enough clothes to dress an army."

"Are you going to send me back to New York?" I asked in a trembling voice. Dad's frown scared me.

"No, I am not," he said, kissing my forehead. "New York has already done enough damage to the Tiffany I used to know. The sooner we get to Australia, the better. I'll be able to show you my way of life, my way of thinking." He gave me a big hug and smiled. "I've got five weeks to convince you I'm right."

Chapter Three

During the entire flight to Sydney, Australia, all fifteen hours of it sitting in a cramped seat wondering if my legs still belonged to me, I thought about what it would be like when I got there. As usual my father had been pretty vague when I'd pestered him for information. All I had gotten out of him was that we'd be driving through Australia, taking pictures of wildlife as we went. Adam had said Dad wanted to follow the route of the first overland expedition to the north coast from Sydney—that expedition, incidentally, did not come back alive—and film a man who hunted crocodiles. We'd be in the outback, the isolated land near the middle of Australia. It sounded like the most inviting trip I'd had since the time I went to have my wisdom teeth removed.

I stared out of the window at the clouds floating cottonlike below us and tried to picture Australia. The only things that came to my mind were kangaroos. But since I didn't know what the countryside was like, I couldn't really picture those kangaroos hopping anywhere. Then I remembered that the rock group Men at Work came from Australia; so I could then imagine kangaroos and Men at Work all hopping around together in a big empty nothing. From the things Adam had said and the sort of stuff my father had packed to take with us, freeze-dried food, mosquito repellent, jungle clothing, and millions of maps, I got the impression that we would be fighting for survival in the middle of that big, empty nothing.

So I was very relieved to land in Sydney and see skyscrapers and elegant houses perched around a glittering blue harbor.

We checked into our hotel, and then Adam and I decided to wander around Sydney while Dad took care of some business.

"This isn't bad at all," I said to Adam. "I think I could possibly survive here."

Just then two beautifully suntanned girls wearing miniskirts and skimpy halter tops walked past Adam and me. They tossed back their long, sun-bleached hair as they laughed. "Oh, it was really beaut!" one said. "You should have been there."

"Yiss?" the other one asked with a funny upturned accent. Then they drifted past us, their wooden sandals clomping on the sidewalk like delicate horses' hooves. They stopped beside a lovely fountain that sprayed out delicate circular patterns of water, like an enormous dandelion.

Adam sighed contentedly. "Yes," he said, "not bad at all. I think I could survive here, too."

We decided to go for a bite at a little outdoor café in Kings Cross, the trendy part of Sydney. All around us were neat little boutiques and record stores. The people who walked past were just as fashionable as those in New York, and the passion fruit ice cream was yummy. We were staying at a Hilton hotel, and we'd passed a McDonald's and a Kentucky Fried Chicken. If there was any difference between Sydney and New York City, it was only that lots of men wore shorts to work. They were very elegant shorts, worn with short-sleeved shirts and ties, and the men looked cool and relaxed, which is more than New York businessmen ever do in summer.

Oh, and speaking of summer, when I had pestered Dad and Adam for information, neither of them had mentioned that Australia, being on the other side of the earth, has summer when we have winter. That little fact came as a terrible shock as soon as the heat hit me outside the airport. The worst part was that I'd brought no light clothes with me at all.

"You might have told me it was summer here," I complained to my father. "What am I going to wear?"

My father, who is the least clothes-minded person in the entire world, looked surprised. "I thought everyone knew that Australia's seasons were opposite from those of the United States," he said. "Go buy a couple pair of shorts."

How he thought a girl like me could survive for weeks in "a couple pair of shorts" I don't know. Besides, none of these sophisticated, fashionable Sydney women were wearing shorts around town.

"Tomorrow I've got to do some serious shopping," I said to Adam, who had finished his ice cream and was starting on a large slice of pumpkin pie topped with so much whipped cream that I almost gained a pound just looking at it.

...e thing I had noticed was that both my ...ner and Adam had this funny way of looking at me. It sometimes made me wonder if I was speaking a foreign language. "Tomorrow?" Adam said. "You want to do some shopping tomorrow?"

"Yes, is it some sort of public holiday I don't know about?"

Adam sighed. "Listen, kid, you'd better make the most of Sydney comforts today because the expedition leaves tomorrow."

I didn't like the use of that word "expedition." It conjured up pictures of camel trains in the desert or explorers hacking out paths through the jungle. I remembered those packets of freeze-dried food.

"We leave t-tomorrow?" I stammered.

Adam nodded.

"And how long will we be on this—this 'expedition'?"

"Almost five weeks," Adam said matter-of-factly. "If all goes well," he added.

I didn't like the sound of "if all goes well," either. I was too much of a coward to ask what could not go well. "I think I'll just stay in Sydney and wait for you to come back," I said. "After all, someone's got to keep an eye on the things you leave behind. I'm sure I could survive in the Hilton for a few weeks."

Adam laughed. "I can't see Dad dragging you all the way here and then abandoning you. Besides, he wants you to come. He wants to show you the way we do things. He's really worried that you're turning out just like Mom."

"And what's so wrong with that!" I said. "She's your mother, too, you know. You shouldn't bad-mouth her all the time."

"Oh, come on, Tiffany," Adam said. "You know as well as I do what's wrong with Mom. She fusses over nothing and ignores anything that doesn't fit her way of life. Dad doesn't want you growing up with only her values. Look at the stink you made over that broken fingernail. Dad brought you out here to shape you up!"

"I don't want to be shaped up," I said. "I happen to like me just the way I am."

"Too bad," Adam said. "Because I have a feeling you are going to be shaped up, whether you like it or not."

He got up, left some money on the table, and walked away down the hill, leaving me to follow along seething with anger. Why had I been looking forward to seeing my father and brother again? They were both obnoxious, completely and utterly obnoxious! What made them think they were the only people in the world who knew how to live? Just because they didn't like my mother's way of life didn't mean theirs was any better.

"Not everyone in the world has to like chasing animals and climbing mountains!" I called after Adam. "And I happen to think that living in a neat house is healthier than living in the mess you two do!" Adam just turned around and grinned, which made me even angrier.

We met my father downstairs in the hotel. He had an armful of maps and travel guides and looked very pleased with himself. "It's all arranged. I've just left Mick Dawson," he said. "He's our backer, a rich Australian who has made millions in wool and is now putting a lot of money into saving wildlife. He's paying for the entire expedition. The vehicles are ready, and we start early tomorrow."

"What are we traveling on, camels?" I asked bitterly.

"She's not looking forward to coming along," Adam told Dad. "She'd rather stay behind in the Hilton and wait for us."

My father frowned at me. "You're coming, my girl, and that is that. By the end of this trip, you're going to be a different person. Have you had time to get her any boots yet, Adam?"

"Boots?" I yelled loudly enough for people

38

sitting in the lobby to turn around and stare. "We're not going mountain climbing, too, are we?"

"No, but you need boots for walking through the bush," my father said.

"I've got a perfectly good pair of Nikes for walking," I said. "Boots would make my feet hot, and I want to get nice brown ankles."

"Suit yourself," my father said. "I'm sure all the snakes will be really understanding. I'll just get Adam to walk ahead of you and shout, 'Don't bite her, she's trying to get a tan on her ankles.'"

I glared at Dad, but I was so scared about meeting a snake that I went with Adam and bought boots. They were light canvas and came up to my knees.

"Of course, if the snake is up in a tree to start with, these won't help much," the little man in the store said, then laughed loudly. I glared at him, too. I felt as if I were in the middle of a nightmare from which I couldn't wake up. Was it only a few days before that I had been in a fashionable New York suburb, living in an elegant house, and going to school with my friends?

Oh, Greg, I thought now as I walked down the scorching Sydney street clutching my new boots. *Have you forgotten me already? Are*

you going to that dance with somebody else?
I wondered if everyone else had forgotten about
me, too. Were Becky and Elizabeth and the
rest discussing how I was doing, or had I
slipped out of their lives without a trace? And
what about my mother? As she lounged on
that deck beside Felix and sipped her cool
drink, did she ever think about the daughter
she had abandoned? Had she had any idea
about the fate she was condemning me to?
Surely she wouldn't have sent me to my father if she'd known I'd end up in the Australian outback.

After we got the boots, my father gave me
some money to go shopping for clothes, but
my heart wasn't really in it. At home clothes
shopping was a major hobby. Even when I
didn't have any money, I spent my weekends
in stores, deciding what I would buy when I
did have some money. But what could I buy
that would go with boots? I thought of all the
cute summer clothes I had at home, mini
outfits, cotton shorts, sun dresses. Then I
sighed heavily and bought myself shorts that
looked like they were from an army surplus
store.

"I hope you're satisfied," I growled to my
father.

He laughed and put his arm around me.

"You're the one who'll be satisfied when we're out in that hundred-degree heat and you feel comfortable. Those are proper tropical shorts. Now you'll look like a real member of the expedition. You should wear them when we go out to dinner tonight."

Dinner was wonderful. We went to a restaurant right at the end of Sydney Harbour and watched the sun setting behind the skyscrapers and turning the water silver and pink. We sat at a little outdoor table and ate lobsters so large they hung over the plates.

Later that night, I looked out of my window on the twenty-ninth floor of the Hilton and saw the lights of the city twinkling below me, and the red line of taillights crossing the Sydney Harbour Bridge. The noises of the city came up to meet me, horns honking, the screech of brakes, and a distant siren. These were the noises I knew. They made me feel secure. I wasn't looking forward to the next day, I thought as I climbed into bed.

Chapter Four

The two other members of the expedition arrived early the next morning, before I was out of bed. Much to my dismay, and his amusement, Adam had told me on the flight over that Dad was filming a straight documentary—there'd be no cute actors, no chance at doing makeup, no nothing. Just us and the miserably rugged Australian outback.

I dressed quickly and joined my father and Adam, who were in front of the hotel sorting mountains of baggage. The gear was being piled onto two Land Rovers by a skinny little old man. His face, the color of old leather, was as wrinkled as a prune. He wore a shapeless, colorless terry cloth hat on his head. He looked up when I arrived and called to me, "Hey, miss, you seen my cobber?"

I looked around me, not knowing what I was looking for. For all I knew, a cobber could have been either an animal or a piece of machinery. "Your what?" I asked.

"My cobber, my mate. The bloke what's with me," he said. He looked at my face, which was still totally blank, then at my father. "A bit simple in the head, is she?" he asked. "Don't she understand English?"

"I'd understand it very well if you'd speak it," I said frostily.

At this, the old man opened his mouth and laughed loudly. I was amazed to see that at least half his teeth were missing. "I can tell you just arrived Down Under," he said. "You can't understand a flamin' word I'm saying, can you. You've got to learn to talk Strine, that's what you've got to learn."

"This is Sam," my father said before I could snap back with a cutting retort. "He's going to be our guide, our handyman, and our cook."

Oh great, I thought with a sinking heart. *I'm not going to have a weight problem on this trip. I'd rather starve than eat anything he cooked.*

"Sam, this is my daughter Tiffany," my father went on pleasantly.

"I reckoned as much," Sam said, giving me

a toothless grin, "seeing as how she looks just like you. Pleased to meet you, miss."

"Here, Tiffany, don't just stand there," my father said. "Go bring down your stuff. I want to get out of here as soon as possible."

It was now the height of rush hour. Smartly dressed people were walking by and giving us strange looks as we piled our weird assortment of baggage in front of the elegant hotel. I squirmed with embarrassment and disappeared into the hotel again. I was overjoyed to get out of there!

I staggered out again with a backpack containing as many clothes as I was able to jam in and the essentials of survival—my makeup kit, my hairbrush, and five candy bars. I had discovered the night before that Australia had some great candy bars, and I was not going to enter the unknown without my survival rations. And now that I'd discovered Sam was to be the cook, my survival rations became even more important. I wondered if I could take two tiny bites of candy a day and make my supply last for five weeks.

I wasn't used to carrying my own stuff. When I traveled with Mom, she always acted helpless; if no strong man came to rescue her, she got a porter. I acted as if my backpack were twice as heavy as it really was and waited for Adam or Sam to take it from me. But they didn't; so I staggered out to the Land Rovers with it.

"Oh, there he is, there's my cobber," Sam called, looking behind me. "Where you been, old mate? Taking a quick break?"

"No chance of that with this slave driver around," said the voice behind me, and a tall blond boy came up to us, carrying a huge bundle on his back.

My father looked up from the knots he was tying and grinned. "That's right, and just you remember it, young man," he said to the boy. "You don't work fast enough, and you'll get the very worst punishment—we ship you back home."

"Oh, anything but that," the boy joked, adding his bundle to the mountain on the Land Rover. So we had a baggage boy as well as a weird old cook. Some expedition!

The boy was standing on the open back of the Land Rover, looking at me with interest. I noticed, to my annoyance, that his eyes were alarmingly blue and that the corners of his mouth curved into a cute little smile. Before I almost weakened and smiled back, I made myself remember that I had sworn I was not going to enjoy a single moment of this expedition. He looked like the conceited type, anyway. Well, I wasn't going to fall for some vain baggage boy.

"Here," I called up to him, "you can come and get this now."

He looked at me as if I were a creature from another planet. *Another weirdo who doesn't understand English*, I thought with a sigh.

"Pardon me?" he asked, confirming my belief that he was an idiot.

"I said you can take my baggage now," I said sharply. "Only be careful with it, I don't want it put where things can get broken."

He tried to stop grinning but couldn't. "Yes, ma'am," he said, reaching down for my backpack.

"Just a minute, Tiffany," my father interrupted. "This young man is—"

"Bruce, miss," the boy interrupted. "I'm helping your father with the expedition. Nice to meet you."

"Nice to meet you, too, Bruce," I said politely, wishing his eyes weren't so very blue and he weren't looking at me with that grin that unnerved me.

"OK. Let's get out of here," my father said, tying a final knot and climbing into the driver's seat of the first vehicle. "We have a long way to go today, and I want to make camp before dark."

It sounded so strange to hear someone saying things like that in the middle of a city, while men and women with briefcases hurried past and buses inched by in traffic. I couldn't imagine making camp in the wilderness while the McDonald's sign still winked at us from across the street. It was almost as if my father were acting the part of expedition leader in a movie.

"Climb in, Tiffany," Dad commanded just as I was deciding to run across and fill my backpack with Big Macs. "You can ride with Adam and Bruce, and Sam can ride with me."

Adam swung himself into the backseat beside a pile of camera equipment, leaving me to climb into the front next to Bruce. Bruce still looked amused, as if he had a secret joke. I wondered again if he was all right in the head. He started the engine, and we crawled into the stream of city traffic, gradually picking up speed as we left the center of the city behind us.

The wind in my face felt good. Bruce turned the radio to a rock station, which cut out any need for conversation, and we relaxed into our seats. Suburbs flashed past us, mostly one-story houses with bright, red-tiled roofs and neat squares of lawn in front. Brilliant red, pink, and purple flowers were growing in the yards and climbing up the houses. After a while the houses thinned out, giving way to small farms shaded by eucalyptus trees. It looked remarkably like California, and I began to feel less worried about facing the dangers of the outback. If it didn't get much worse than this, I could definitely survive. Every now and then we drove through a small town where there was a regular supermarket; it looked like I'd be able to replenish my candy supply.

"We're going to make our first camp in the Blue Mountains," Bruce told me. The Sydney radio station had gradually faded into static, meaning we had to talk occasionally.

"Are they far from here?" I asked.

"We reach the beginning of them in about half an hour," he said. "We'll probably stop for a quick look, then press on to our camp, which is on the far side."

"In half an hour?" I said, surprised. "They can't be very high then. When we used to drive to the Sierras in California, we could see them hours before we reached them."

I peered around in all directions. We had been climbing steadily almost since we left Sydney, a gentle slope that went up and up, but the country hadn't become hilly yet. There were still farms on either side of us, certainly no signs of a mountain range on the horizon.

"These take you by surprise," Bruce said seriously.

"You mean they're inflatable?" I asked coolly. "They only rear up when visitors come near? A tourist gimmick?"

Bruce gave me a quick look, but he didn't say anything. Adam, sitting in the back with the air rushing past him, couldn't hear a thing. We drove through a pretty little town with one main street lined with dusty eucalyptus trees that Bruce called gums, then he brought the Land Rover to a halt in a parking lot.

"Are we stopping for a rest?" I asked. From what my father had said, I thought we were the sort of expedition that drove to the ends of the earth without stopping. This little town looked far too civilized for us.

Bruce had a funny smile on his face. "I've stopped to show you the mountains," he said. "You want to look?"

OK, so this is some dumb Australian joke, I thought as I climbed out. My legs felt stiff, and I was glad to walk. The air felt good, too. It was cool here, crisp and very clear. Almost like mountain air—yet, there was no sign of the famous mountains.

"Which way?" I asked Bruce.

"Over here," he said. "But watch your step."

I walked to the edge of the parking lot, and suddenly Bruce grabbed my arm. "Hey, I said to watch it," he commanded.

I looked down, and suddenly everything began to spin. I stepped back hurriedly from the edge of a sheer drop. I was standing on top of a huge cliff, below me lay an enormous, steep-sided valley. The cliff was yellow rock, the far hills were cloaked in a blue carpet of trees. Absolute silence rose up from the thousand feet below. It was like looking out on a lost planet.

"I forgot to mention," came Bruce's voice in my ear, "that in Australia mountains go down, not up." I realized that he was still holding me tightly and that his face was very close to mine. He was looking at me with an amused sparkle in his eyes. I felt my cheeks flame red, which seemed to amuse him all the more. How dare he act so confident and so much in control with me! Maybe he thought every girl found him irresistible. Well, I, for one, was going to resist.

"You seem to forget who you are," I said icily. "My father hired you; he can just as easily fire you!" I wrenched my arm free and walked away from him. I had expected that last remark to hit home, but it only made him look more amused than ever!

Chapter Five

When we climbed back into the Land Rover, Bruce told Adam it was his turn to drive. I slid hastily into the back directly behind Bruce before he could argue. That way I was out of Bruce's sight, and the open sides of the vehicle made it too noisy for me to be included in the conversation. I was determined to ignore Bruce until I could ask my father to tell him to quit bothering me.

We drove out of town and through a thick gum forest. There were no more signs of farms or villages. We were now entering the real bush, as they called it. Every now and then Bruce turned around and passed on a snippet of information to me, yelling above the roar of the engine that the mountains had been a barrier for early settlers and that many explorers had been lost until it was discovered that the only way to cross the mountains was by the summits.

"Fascinating!" I muttered to myself, scowling at the backs of their necks. Then we turned off the paved road, and the car bumped and jolted its way along a sandy trail that zigzagged back and forth down the steep mountain side. Adam didn't slow down at all, and a huge cloud of dust rose up all around us. Because I was in the open back, I got most of it, and I was soon coughing and sputtering.

"You all right back there?" Bruce called, turning around to me and grinning again.

I was about to make a sarcastic comment about how I liked suffocating and having my back broken at the same time, but then I remembered that I was ignoring him. "I'm fine, thank you," I said stiffly.

"You can come up here with us, if you like," he yelled. "There's plenty of room!"

"I'd rather shave my head," I muttered in the back.

The bush flashed past, unchanging, and the dust floated behind us like a long yellow ribbon. Just when I was wondering if my back could survive another jolt, Adam pointed ahead and called out, "They made it ahead of us."

A wisp of smoke was rising through the trees, and we could see the sun glinting on metal.

"We were lucky to get permission for this site," Bruce said. "This is the middle of bushfire season, and it's particularly dry this year. They aren't allowing any open fires at all, just barbeques in the brick pits. Not that it helps much. When the gum trees get dry enough, they just explode by themselves."

I looked around nervously at the several million gum trees and wondered when one of them might choose to explode. Bruce saw my nervous expression. "Don't worry," he said. "This isn't good bushfire weather. You'll know it when it comes. If the south wind comes through in a day or so, you can start worrying."

"A lot of comfort you are," I muttered as we bumped into camp.

My father already had a camera set up and was filming Sam cooking steaks over charcoal. He greeted us with a halfhearted wave, then went right back to his filming.

"Come on, Tiffany," Adam called. "Help get out the stuff for tonight. It's in our Land Rover."

"Where are we going to put the tents?" I asked.

Adam and Bruce both seemed to find this funny. "What do you think this is, a Girl Scout outing?" Adam asked, teasing me.

"I don't see what's so funny about that," I said angrily. "I thought when you went camping, you slept in tents."

"You only need a tent to protect you from bad weather," Bruce said. "A sleeping bag is all we need here."

"But what about animals and things?" I blurted out. That made them both laugh again.

"You mean all the fierce wombats and possums," Adam said.

"How am I supposed to know what dangerous animals there are?" I snapped. "I only just got here. I didn't want to come, and before this I hardly knew that Australia existed. Anyway, you made me buy those huge boots. What about snakes? I don't want one in my sleeping bag."

"A snake could just as easily get in your tent," Bruce said. Why didn't I find that remark comforting?

Needless to say, I did not sleep well that night. I had my sleeping bag pulled so tightly over my head that I could hardly breathe, and I kept imagining that things were creeping over me. The night was full of noises. There were rustles and squeaks and squawks and even the crackling of twigs as something walked past us. When I poked my head out, I couldn't see anything. The others were all snoring peacefully, and I felt as if I were guarding the entire camp—alone.

I suppose I drifted off to sleep around two o'clock because the next thing I knew, a maniac was laughing hysterically right above my head. I shot my eyes open. It was light, and I could see the delicate pattern of the eucalyptus leaves against the clear sky. I looked around, but the clearing was still totally peaceful. Then that terrible laughter came again, this time joined by someone playing the flute badly.

There has to be some logical explanation for this, I told myself. *Either I am in the middle of a nightmare and I haven't woken up yet, or this place is possessed by ghosts. Or there really is a madman laughing and another one playing the flute.* None of those explanations made me feel any better.

At that moment somebody yawned loudly, and the noises stopped as if by magic. Bruce sat up in his sleeping bag and looked across to me. "G'day!" he said, which seemed to be the Australian version of hi. "Sleep well?"

I wasn't about to tell him how frightened I had been all night. "OK, I guess," I said, "until someone started laughing and someone else began playing the flute. Did you hear them? Who could be making those noises out in the middle of nowhere?"

Bruce laughed. He seemed to spend a lot of his time laughing at me. Personally, I didn't think I was at all funny. "Kookaburra and maggies," he said.

"What?" I asked. "Can you translate that into English?"

"The sounds you heard," he said, "weren't people at all, they were birds. The one that laughs is the kookaburra, and the one that sounds like weird music is the magpie."

Just then a phone rang loudly in the tree above us. "And I suppose that's a bird, too," I said.

He nodded. "Bellbird."

"It figures," I said. "Do they have telephone-shaped beaks?"

"It's hard to see a bellbird," he said, "because they're small and brown; so they're sort of camouflaged. But I can point out a kookaburra if you want, and the maggies will probably come and show themselves when they find out there's food around." He climbed out of his sleeping bag. "You want to see the kookaburra?" he asked.

"Don't you listen to him, miss," came Sam's voice from his sleeping bag. "That's what all Australian blokes say when they want to lure a pretty girl into the bush."

"Hey, Sam," Bruce said, laughing, "now you've given away my entire plan. Why don't you get on with breakfast instead of listening in on other people's conversations!"

"All right, I'm moving," Sam grumbled, rising out of his bag and putting his old hat on his head. "But don't say I didn't warn you, miss," he called as he shuffled off toward the barbeque pit.

In the end my father and Adam came with us to see the kookaburra, lugging a portable camera and sound equipment. We found two of them, sitting on a low branch. They looked as if they were straight out of a Walt Disney movie, with high foreheads, fluffy feathers, and dark, intelligent eyes. They sat there, not the least bit worried that four strangers were staring at them, and chuckled as if they were telling each other jokes. As we finally turned to leave, one of them gave a loud burst of laughter as if the joke were really on us.

"They weren't frightened of us at all," I commented to my father.

"You'll find that with Australian birds," Bruce said before my father could answer. "Most of them are very curious, and they'll come quite close to people. Out here in the bush, they don't see too many human beings, and so they haven't learned to be afraid."

When we got back to camp, we found that Bruce was right about the magpies, too. Several of them had arrived, big black-and-white birds the size of ravens, and were strutting around behind Sam's back. Every now and then, one of them would open its mouth and out would come the strange flute sounds. I felt as if I were in the middle of a cartoon in which animals could sing or talk.

"Shut up, will you," Sam yelled at them and flung them a piece of meat. They all pounced on it, fighting until they tore it to shreds. "Grub up," Sam said to us. "Get yourselves plates."

Then, to my utter horror, Sam dropped a huge steak with a fried egg sitting on top onto my plate. I am not really a breakfast person. A slice of toast or a bowl of Cheerios is the most I can ever manage.

"Sam, I can't eat this," I protested.

"Course you can," he said. "You need to put a bit of flesh on those bones. A good camp breakie will keep you going all day."

59

I struggled through a little bit of the steak and most of the egg, but I threw away Sam's disgusting, very strong tea that he made in an old can. He caught me doing it, too. "Don't know what's good for you, you don't," he said. "I've been drinking my billie tea every day for the last sixty-five years, and I ain't had a day's sickness in my life." I decided privately that any virus would be very wise to stay away from Sam's tea, but that wasn't a good enough reason for me to drink it.

After breakfast we packed in a hurry and left. My father wanted to reach a koala sanctuary before nightfall. It was a beautiful morning. Even I, who had made a vow not to like anything, had to admit that it was perfect. The sky was a transparent light blue, like tinted glass. The orange dirt road stretched out ahead of us, colored by the delicate shadows the gum trees threw.

When we came upon a tree full of giant white flowers, I called out in amazement, "What are those flowers?" Then I remembered I wasn't speaking to Bruce. At the sound of my voice, the flowers rose into the air and flapped lazily to another tree, squawking as they went.

"Those flowers were cockatoos," Bruce said, looking delighted at my mistake.

Later we passed a lot of pink parrots feeding beside the road and then some little green parakeets. I didn't comment on either of them in case they turned out to be flowers in parrot shape.

"We haven't seen a single kangaroo yet," I said at last. "I thought Australia was full of kangaroos. I expected to see them bounding across the roads all the time." I had hardly said the last word when it happened. Adam jammed on the brakes as three large, brown shapes shot from the bush on our right and in two enormous bounces disappeared into the bush on our left, moving so fast they were almost a blur.

"I think you requested kangaroos," Bruce started to say when something happened. A fourth kangaroo leaped across after the others, and as it landed on the bank on the opposite side, something came flying out of her pocket, did a somersault, and landed on the road. The kangaroo didn't even slow down but disappeared into the thick undergrowth. In a second Bruce leaped from his seat.

"What is it?" Adam yelled after him.

"She dropped her baby," he yelled back. Adam climbed out. I did, too. The baby kangaroo was lying in the road, not moving. It was about a foot long and seemed to be all legs.

"Is it dead?" I asked.

"I doubt it," Bruce said, kneeling down and lifting it up very gently. "They're very tough." As he finished speaking, the baby wriggled in his hands.

"Should you be touching him?" Adam asked. "Won't the mother reject him after that?"

Bruce looked up and frowned. "She won't come back for him," he said. "Once a baby gets thrown out, it would be a miracle if its mother found it again."

"So what happens to them?" I asked. The little kangaroo had lifted its head and was looking around with big, scared eyes.

"They usually don't survive," he said. "A dingo will get to them or a big bird of prey."

"You're not going to leave this one here to die?" I pleaded.

He frowned again. "Of course not. We'll take it with us to the animal keeper at the koala sanctuary. I just hope it's old enough to eat solid food. They're a terrible nuisance to bottle-feed."

My father's vehicle arrived at that moment, and Bruce had to explain the whole thing over again. While we talked, the baby became very upset, kicking and wriggling in Bruce's hands. "I hope the poor little thing doesn't die of fright or exhaustion," Dad said.

"We need to put it in a pouch like its mother's," Bruce said. "Tiffany, go empty your backpack. It's the perfect size."

"Empty out my stuff? Into what?"

"I don't care, onto the floor. Just let me get this little thing comfortable."

"But I've got all my makeup and clothes in there. I can't empty it onto the floor. Can't you find something else?"

"We haven't got all day, and it's the only thing that's the right size. Just tip that stuff out, for heaven's sakes," Bruce snapped. "Come on, Tiffany, you're holding things up. Do you want this baby to die?"

I looked up at him angrily. He was standing there, completely in command, giving me orders. "And who do you think you are?" I asked in my most superior voice. "Just when does a baggage boy give orders to the boss's daughter?"

There was a moment of silence. "Now wait a minute, Tiffany," my father said. "I think it's about time you knew that—"

"No, that's OK, Mr. Johns, just forget it," Bruce interrupted.

"No, Bruce, she's got to know," my father cut in.

"Got to know what?" I asked angrily.

"Tiffany, this is Bruce Dawson," my father said slowly. Dawson—why did that name ring a bell? "You know Mr. Dawson, the person who's financing our expedition? This is his son. Bruce is helping out as a favor because he enjoys being here and because he knows so much about Australian wildlife."

I felt my cheeks become flame red. What a snobby fool I'd made of myself!

Chapter Six

The first thing I noticed when we went into the cabin at the koala reserve was a huge calendar on the wall. On it was a bright picture of Queen Elizabeth in all her robes with a crown on her head. The days were crossed off until that day's date. I stared at the calendar almost as if I were seeing a ghost. The last time I'd looked at a calendar was the day before Greg invited me to the dance. Had it really been less than a week ago that I'd been in New York, surrounded by my friends, knowing where I was and where I was going? As I looked around the primitive, wood-paneled room, at the backpack with the baby kangaroo in it, at the other members of the expedition, all dusty from the long drive, my old life seemed like another world, a half-forgotten dream.

I was shaken out of my thoughts as Bob, the warden, a tall, suntanned man of about thirty, came toward me. "Is this the joey you found?" he asked.

"Pardon me?" I asked. Whoever thought Australia was an English-speaking country had never tried to talk to people there.

"The joey," he repeated, taking my backpack from me as if I were a helpless child.

"They call baby kangaroos joeys," Bruce told me. He didn't seem in the least embarrassed by my terrible mistake earlier. He had wanted my father to drop the whole thing, but Dad had had a few choice words to say about treating all people politely, no matter who they were. The words still stung now, and I had to admit that he was right. Living with my mother, I had gotten used to snapping my fingers for taxis and having a doorman carry up my bags. I guess I had begun to think I was superior in some way. I felt absolutely ashamed of myself.

Bob took the baby kangaroo out of the backpack and checked it over. "It'll survive," he said. "But I bet it could do with a drink. Go take it out to my wife in the outhouse. She's the animal keeper. Get her to fix you a bottle for it." Then, to my horror, he handed the joey back to me. I was about to protest that I didn't know a thing about feeding baby kangaroos, but the guys all walked out before I could open my mouth. I was left with a kicking, squirming bundle in my hands.

The animal keeper was in a cool stone building, trying to feed several baby kangaroos who hopped behind her as she walked back and forth across the floor. She looked up and pushed her long blond hair out of her eyes as I came in.

"Oh, heavens, not another one!" she exclaimed. "It's like a kangaroo epidemic this year. That one doesn't look like it's old enough to eat yet. I'll get it a bottle in a minute." Then she hurried on across the room with the baby kangaroos all hopping behind her. At the door she turned around. "I'm Kay, by the way," she said. "You must think me very rude, but we seem to be snowed under with animals at the moment, and they all want to be fed at the same time."

"Can I help at all?" I heard myself say to my own astonishment.

A broad smile crossed her face. "That would be lovely," she said. "Here, just put down this pail. That'll keep this lot quiet, and we'll go and make the bottles."

I must admit it was a strange feeling to have a dozen or so baby kangaroos hopping hopefully after me. It was even stranger to sit with a baby kangaroo in my lap and feed him from a bottle. I began to understand why Adam had always kept pets. It felt good to take care of something that was helpless. I remembered suddenly the hamster I had had when I was eight and how upset I had been when it died.

In the middle of feeding the kangaroo, at the stage when I had gotten more milk down the front of my shirt than down its throat, Adam and Bruce walked in.

"You're not supposed to bathe in it," Adam said with a grin.

"Well, you do it then if you're so smart," I snapped, feeling uneasy with Bruce standing there.

"Yes, you should try it, Adam," Bruce cut in. "They're the most annoying creatures to feed. They're so greedy they can't wait to get the bottle in their mouths, and then they spill most of it. You're doing a great job, Tiffany."

I think it was the first time he used my name. Anyway, I looked up from the baby kangaroo and met his eyes. This time they weren't amused. He looked at me as if he understood. For a long moment we stared at each other. Why was he being so nice to me, especially after how stupid I'd sounded that morning? How could I ever feel at ease with Bruce after what I'd said?

That night we slept in the cabin. Strangely enough I wished we could have slept outside because the night was unbearably hot. I tossed and turned, got up, splashed myself all over with cold water, and went to stand at the open window, but there was not a breath of wind to cool me down.

In the morning I woke to find a wind had sprung up, but it wasn't a cooling wind. It came roaring through the mountains, hot as a furnace, and it smelled of smoke. The animals around the compound moved about uneasily.

"Is there a fire somewhere?" I asked Bob when I met him outside the house.

He nodded. "About twenty miles away, so they say on the radio. It's in a populated area, and they think they've got it under control. But with this wind, well, you never know."

We had breakfast in the kitchen, then headed out to film the koalas. Since these were wild koalas, I had thought they might be hard to find and film. But Bob led us straight to them.

"How did you find them so easily?" I asked. He laughed, but already I was not quite so sensitive about people laughing at me.

"They're very lazy animals," he said. "If you find a koala sleeping in a certain tree one day, there's a darned good chance he'll be sleeping in the same tree the next day."

"I wish we could see one up close," I said.

"Do you want to hold one?" Bob asked, and before I could answer, he walked across to a tree, pulled down a sleeping koala, and put it in my arms. It didn't even struggle, but clung to me like a living teddy bear while my father filmed us.

"Well, I suppose this is one way to break into movies," I said, laughing.

We photographed all day. The koalas were very cute and cuddly but extremely stupid. When we'd put one down, it would only go as far as the nearest tree, climb up to the first limb, and go to sleep again.

"You have to be a bit careful of the males," Bob explained. "They aren't so good tempered, and they'll bite if they get annoyed."

By the end of the day, my father was delighted with the film he had shot. There wasn't much action because the koalas didn't budge unless we moved them, but they allowed us to get fantastic close-ups. Even the babies weren't playful but clung to their mothers' backs, half asleep. Feeling hot and tired, we drove back to the compound. The wind was as strong as ever and still smelled of smoke. We fell asleep uneasily.

I woke from a deep, dreamless sleep to the sound of voices outside. Footsteps were running over gravel. I staggered over to my window. It was still dark, and a heavy, golden moon hung in the sky.

"What's happening?" I called to the first figure who ran past me.

"The fire's jumped a valley and is heading in this direction," Bruce yelled. "We've got to get the koalas moved."

"What about us?" I wanted to ask. "How about getting us moved to safety?" Instead, I made myself act cool and calm. I dressed in a hurry and ran out to join them. I didn't really have time to ask myself what I was doing before we had jumped into Bob's Land Rover and were bumping over the dirt trail toward the koalas.

The fire was a reality now, not just a hint of smoke on the breeze, but a dull red glow. It was just a valley away, roaring and crackling and coming toward us. I was so scared I actually felt sick. I didn't dare speak because I didn't trust my voice. Could a Land Rover outrun a fire? I wondered. If the flames had jumped a valley, what if they jumped another one and we were cut off? The others all looked so cool and efficient. Why on earth hadn't I stayed behind? I had a good excuse, I could have helped Kay with the baby animals.

The night was so dark. The Land Rover's headlights cut a thin beam of light through the blackness, and trees loomed up alarmingly close on either side of us. I don't know how Bob managed to drive so fast, but we seemed to fly along that trail, engine roaring. We were bounced up and down with every bump in the road. This didn't do my nervous stomach much good, either. Nobody spoke, but then the engine's roar was so loud that we would have had to shout. When we screeched to a halt and Bob turned off the engine, the silence was almost complete. Only the distant crackle of the fire beyond the ridge broke the stillness.

"Here, hold these," Bob said, handing two large flashlights to my father and brother. "You shine them on the koalas, and Bruce and I will bring them down with the pole."

"Anything you want me to do?" I asked, hoping he would say no.

"My word, yes!" he said. "We're going to need you to help us get them into the sacks."

I didn't like to say I'd rather have held the flashlight. I remembered all too clearly that the males could give a nasty bite. I could see the headline now—"GIRL DIES OF RABIES AFTER BAD KOALA BITES." Still, even that was slightly better than "GIRL BURNED TO DEATH TRYING TO RESCUE KOALAS," which looked as if it, too, might be a possiblity. The dull red glow seemed to get brighter by the minute. The smell of smoke was making my eyes water.

We reached the trees, and my father and brother played the flashlights over them. I didn't see a single koala. "Oh, no," Bob said with a sigh. "They've chosen tonight of all nights to move on to a new feeding ground."

"Would they have moved far?" Adam asked, sweeping his light through the surrounding trees.

"No, not far, but there are an awful lot of trees in this forest, and I'd hate to search through every one in a hurry."

Suddenly Adam called out, "Here's one," and we found them just a few trees away. The only problem was, those trees were much taller and the koalas were all out of reach. The warden picked off the lowest one with his long pole. The pole had a noose on the end, and Bob just hooked it around the koala's neck, then jerked it backward. The poor thing came flying to the ground and landed with a terrible thud.

"Won't that hurt them?" I asked, opening a sack while he stuffed the koala in.

"Not so much as being burned to death," he said grimly. Then he smiled at me. "Don't worry, they've got well-padded behinds."

The rest of the koalas were alert now. They had seen what had happened to their friend and climbed higher into the branches.

"I'll climb up for you," Bruce volunteered. "I used to shinny up trees taller than this when I was a kid."

"Well, take care you don't get bitten," Bob said. "And don't take any risks. You know how brittle those branches are."

We watched Bruce swing himself up into the enormous gum tree and disappear among the foliage. It seemed only seconds later that we heard him call, "Here comes one," and a furry shape came flying through the air. Bob managed to break this one's fall, and we got it into the sack with no fuss. In fact, the whole operation seemed to be going smoothly. Bruce cleared one tree of bears and went up the next.

Then, all of a sudden, there was a great

cracking sound, a shout, and a large limb crashed to earth. "I can't get at most of them," Bruce's voice yelled down. "They're all up on the smaller branches at the top. Those limbs just won't hold my weight."

"Are there a lot up there?" Bob called back.

"At least a dozen."

"Then that's the whole troop," Bob said. He turned to me. "How are you at climbing trees?" he asked.

"Me?" I asked in horror.

"You don't weigh much. I thought maybe you could get higher than Bruce."

No, I wanted to yell. I don't want to be here at all. I don't like this sort of thing. I'm scared. I want to go home.

"You can do it, Till," my father said gently. "You used to be a great tree climber when you were a kid."

"Well, OK, I'll try," I said very doubtfully.

I walked over to the big tree. Its bark was peeling off in great shreds, and it didn't look very inviting at all. Dad lifted me to where I could grab the first limb, and I pulled myself up into the middle of the leaves. As the first leaves brushed my face, I remembered about snakes and spiders and bugs. Did snakes sleep at night? They would surely wake up if a large human stepped on them by mistake, wouldn't they? I pushed these worries to the back of my mind. I had other things to think about right then.

Bruce saw me coming, reached his hand down to me, and gave me a big smile. "Good climbing, mate," he said. "See where most of them are, up that branch? It just wouldn't take my weight. I'll try and steady you all the way. Just grab them by the back of the neck and drop them down. If you lose the surprise factor, they'll cling on to the tree, and you won't be able to move them."

At that moment the fire broke over the ridge. A great burst of flame shot into the night sky, and the dull roar became a close, immediate crackling.

"How long do we have?" I asked nervously.

"I don't know. Just grab the ones you can," Bruce answered. "Bob will tell us when we have to leave. He's been through a lot of these fires."

I wriggled my way up the branch and found a koala wedged in a fork. I had forgotten how big they were. As I tried to snatch it from the branch, I could feel its full weight. Finally, I wrenched it free and tried to hold it and clutch on to the branch at the same time. For one sickening second, I swung out on the branch one-handed. Bruce grabbed at my shirt, and

I swung back and steadied myself. The koala, of course, was frightened and clung to me with its very sharp claws. I held it around the middle and called shakily. "I've got one."

"Just drop it," Bruce yelled to me.

I let it fall and grabbed the next one. This one had a baby on her back, and she bit me. "I've got a baby up here, I don't want to drop it," I yelled down.

"We'll hold out the sack, try and aim for it," Bob shouted, "and then come down. That fire's moving fast."

I let go of the two koalas and didn't even wait to see if they made the sack safely before I grabbed another and dropped it. I could see a little group of koalas huddled together, looking at me with big, scared eyes. But they were all out of reach.

"If someone could pass me up a pole, I could get them," I yelled.

"No time, Tiffany, come on down," my father shouted.

"We have to leave them, Tiffany," Bruce said, pulling at me. The group of little faces peered down at me with their big eyes.

"No, we can't just leave them," I called back. "Let me see if that branch will hold me."

"It won't, and I won't let you try," Bruce said. He grabbed my waist and pulled me down beside him. "Climb down right now. If we don't get moving, we won't get out of here."

As he spoke, a tree across the clearing burst into flame with a loud explosion.

"Why don't the koalas try and get away?" I shouted.

"They're just too stupid," he yelled back. "Now hurry."

I made myself climb down, my fingers slipping along the peeling bark, until I was grabbed by my father and Bob and flung into the Land Rover. Its engine was already revving, and we drove off like mad things just as the trees behind us burst into flame.

The fire exploded around us with a frightening roar. We could feel the heat licking at us. Smoke swirled everywhere, making us choke. I don't know how Bob managed to find his way back along that narrow, twisting trail, but somehow, we were outrunning the fire. I had been scared silly when we started out. Now I felt numb. I sat like a statue between Bruce and Adam in the back, not turning around to see if the flames were catching us, not speaking, not even crying. I felt as if I had been squeezed too hard and all the life had been pressed out of me.

We had almost made it back to the camp when we were met by headlights on the trail ahead. "We were just about to come and look for you," a voice yelled as we slowed to a halt. "Thought you were getting yourselves cooked up there. Kay was quite frantic."

"We managed to get a few koalas," Bob called back, sounding as if he were chatting with a neighbor over the back fence, not as if he had just managed to escape a fire. "But we weren't quick enough to get them all."

"Pity," the other voice said. "Still, it can't be helped. We're about to start a back-burn. Get in the house."

We pulled into the yard. Several fire trucks were parked there, and fire fighters were hurrying about, yelling things to each other.

"What are they doing?" Adam asked.

"They're going to back burn," Bob said, grabbing a couple of wriggling sacks of koalas and staggering toward the outhouse with them. "They'll start a small fire here to meet the main fire. That way, the main fire won't come in our direction."

"What if the wind changes?" Adam asked.

"Then things will get pretty hot," Bob said calmly. "That's a risk we have to take out here."

Adam and Bruce took the sacks of koalas

and hurried after Bob. My father had his camera going and was filming the whole thing. I just stood there in the yard, forgotten for the moment. I couldn't make myself move. I didn't even know where I wanted to go. My throat was burning from the smoke, and my eyes were stinging badly, but I couldn't move. I watched the flames of the back-burn spring up in a line and race away from us toward the far-off glow.

How many more koalas are sitting in trees out there? I thought. *How many other little animals are watching the fire come toward them and don't know what to do about it?*

"Hey, Tiffany," Bruce called to me. "Tiffany, are you all right?"

He came over to me and put a hand on my shoulder. "Come on inside," he said gently. "You don't want to keep breathing in this smoke. Kay's made tea." He started to lead me gently. "You did a great job out there," he said.

Suddenly it was as if something inside me snapped. "We didn't do a great job. We left most of them to burn!" I yelled.

He turned toward me and put both hands on my shoulders. "We did all we could," he said. "What would have been the sense in staying up there too long and getting killed ourselves?"

Tears were starting to roll down my cheeks, one after the other. "But those poor little animals," I said, completely choked up. "They were just sitting there waiting for me to help them." I swallowed back the sobs and wiped away my tears with the back of my hand. "I'm sorry," I said stiffly. "I'm acting like a baby."

"No, you're not," Bruce said. He put his arm around me and led me across to a little sheltered porch where he sat me down beside him. "It's all right to cry, you know," he said. "You've been scared—we all have. And you've been shocked, too. Go ahead and cry. See, I'll even provide a shoulder." And he put my face gently against his shirt.

Then I couldn't stop the tears coming. "Oh, Bruce," I said sobbing. "I feel so terrible. I can still see those eyes looking down at me, waiting for me to do something. And I left them all to be burned. . . ."

He was stroking my hair. "But we saved some, Tiff," he said. "That's better than nothing, isn't it? Even if we'd only managed to save one, that would have been better than nothing. If it hadn't been for you, all of them in that second tree would have died. You were terrific. I'm proud of you."

I managed a watery smile. "Thanks," I said. "I feel like such a fool. The way I behaved to you before and then crying tonight—"

"Don't you cry much?" he asked, wiping a tear from my cheek with his fingertip.

"I sort of got out of the habit," I said, realizing that I hadn't really cried since the divorce. I had cried so much then. I had been so hurt that I had made up my mind never to be hurt again, I had simply shut out feelings—until that night.

"Well, I'm glad you've gotten back into it," he said. "Crying's a good thing to do when you're sad." He smiled and gave me a wonderful hug. "You know, I think I had you all wrong." He looked at me seriously. I could see his face glowing in the light of the fire. "I thought you were one of those stuck-up sort of girls who only cares about herself and how she looks. I certainly never thought I'd see you sitting here crying for koalas."

"I think I had myself all wrong, too," I said quietly. "And I'm so sorry about—"

"No!" Bruce said firmly, putting a finger on my lips. "No more apologizing. Everything that happened before tonight is forgotten, understood?"

I even managed to smile. "Understood," I said.

"All right, mate," he said with a wink. "Now, let's go in and get that tea." With his arm around my shoulder, we walked toward the cabin.

Chapter Seven

The next morning there was nothing but blackened stumps where the forest had been, stumps that pointed like accusing fingers at the clear sky. Far off, smoke still curled up from smoldering trees. It was like a scene in a movie after a terrible battle. All around was complete silence, no more birds or insects. Even the wind was still.

I walked out of the front door and stood looking at the desolation. It was a depressing scene, and I should have felt terrible. But I didn't. I felt as if I had been reborn, as if I had been living in a prison cell for years and had finally managed to unlock the door. I had done some serious thinking the night before, and I realized that in New York I was always trying to be somebody else. All the interest I'd taken in clothes and my appearance was to stop me from feeling and thinking about things that mattered. Now that I was among real people again, my father, Adam, Bruce, even friendly, crazy old Sam, I was getting things back in perspective. I hadn't been allowing myself to show any emotions because I had no one to turn to who would understand. But Bruce had understood—he had helped to break the spell and turn me around.

I stood there, remembering how good it felt to have his strong arms around me, how he had stroked my hair. Suddenly I heard his voice. "Well, good morning. I must say, you look as if you've just spent a wild night!"

"I do?" I asked, turning around to watch him walk toward me.

He nodded. "Wrestling with a grizzly bear, at least."

I hadn't looked in my makeup mirror for at least four days, which would be amazing for any girl my age, but for me it was a world record.

"Come with me," Bruce said. He took my hand as if it were the most natural thing in the world and led me to the stone outhouse. He opened a small cabinet I hadn't noticed before, and inside it was a mirror. I stared in horror at the person who looked out at me. Where was the model-to-be who never left the house unless her hair and makeup were perfect? The time in the sun had left my nose red and peeling, my cheeks freckled. My hair was curling every which way. I had a scratch down one side of my face, and my arms and legs looked as if I had, indeed, wrestled with a grizzly bear.

"Oh, heavens," I said, putting my hand up to my cheek. "If my mother could see me now." I giggled as I said it, but I couldn't help thinking about whether I would ever really feel at home with Mom and her life-style again, now that I had had a taste of a different world.

"We'd better put some cream on those cuts," Bruce said. "It's too bad we didn't get to it last night, but I suppose there were other things to think about then."

He took a bottle and some cotton out of the cabinet and dabbed antiseptic on all the cuts he could find. It made them all sting, but I wasn't going to complain. I was enjoying every moment of having him stand close and look so concerned about me.

"Up bright and early?" came Bob's voice behind us, and he walked into the room carrying two buckets. "That's good, I need willing helpers again. I've got a whole zoo of animals that need care right now."

"No rest for the weary," Bruce said and gave me a special look. We followed Bob out.

All morning we hardly stopped working. Everyone in the area knew about the sanctuary and had been bringing in frightened or burned animals, casualties of the fire. We had to hold them while Bob put antibiotic powder on burned paws or tails. And let me tell you, they weren't at all grateful. The koalas tried to bite us, and the kangaroos thrashed and wriggled dangerously. By the end of the morning, we had a whole new batch of scratches to add to the old ones. My father was absolutely delighted because he got some terrific film footage of the whole fire episode.

"Just hold its head up a bit there," he kept telling us. "Turn it around toward the camera."

"That's OK for you to say," I'd yell back. "You're just holding a camera, which doesn't bite or kick. You come and take over the kangaroo, and I'll hold the camera for you." But it was good-natured teasing, and when we all stopped for lunch, we felt we had done an important job. We had lunch under the big ghost gum tree beside the house, which mercifully had escaped the fire. We were just getting down to the serious business of eating cold meat pies and sausage rolls when we heard the sound of a helicopter overhead coming closer and closer.

"Probably a government team here to inspect the damage," Bob said, peering into the sky.

"It doesn't look like a government helicopter to me," Kay said, shading her eyes to look up into the bright light. "Looks more like one of those press helicopters."

Bob sighed. "That's the last thing we want right now—reporters! Remember the last time we had a fire? They wanted to go into all the gory details, how many animals were killed, how many burned terribly. And they got in our way when we tried to work."

"Well, it looks like you're going to have to go through all that again," Sam said, "because it's definitely landing here."

The helicopter circled lower and lower, sending a spray of black dust from the burned-out forest over us as it landed. The noise was deafening. We grabbed at the tablecloth as it threatened to fly away and dump all our food on the ash-covered ground. Then the engine died, and the blade turned idly before stopping completely. The copter door opened.

We had been expecting some tough news

reporter to climb out, but instead, a gorgeous girl, not much older than I, swung gracefully to the ground. She had long, almost white, silky hair, and was wearing pale pink shorts and a matching halter top. Standing in the midst of the blackened ruin, she looked like the good fairy on an emergency call. She glanced around with interest, tossed back that wonderful hair, and walked smoothly toward us. She scanned our group through her big, round sunglasses, and then her face broke into a smile.

"Surprise, darling!" she said, showing a mouthful of even, white teeth.

Bruce came around the table to meet her. "What on earth are you doing here, Pamela?" he asked.

"I was worried about you," she said smoothly. "When I heard about the fire on the radio, I said to Daddy, 'I do hope he hasn't done anything stupid, like try to rescue some silly animals and gotten himself trapped.' In fact, I got so upset that in the end Daddy told me I could take the helicopter and make sure you were all right."

"I'm all right," he said, "as you can see."

"But you have some terrible cuts and burns," she said. "Shouldn't you fly out with me and see a doctor?"

"I got a few scratches last night when we were rescuing koalas," Bruce said with a grin, "but mine are nothing compared to Tiffany's."

Pamela's gaze moved along the line of people until she came to me. I couldn't see her eyes because of her sunglasses, but I could feel her disdainful gaze anyway. I was horribly aware that my nose was peeling, that I was covered with scratches and soot, and that I must have looked a real mess.

"Well, darling, I expect she's used to it," Pamela said, looking me up and down as if I were in a zoo. "But you're not. I do wish you would leave all this horrible outdoor stuff to the professionals and not get yourself all scratched and dirty and in danger."

"You know very well that I like it, Pamela," Bruce said. "Otherwise I wouldn't do it. Now, will you go home and tell everybody I'm fine?"

From the moment she had arrived, I had a horrible sinking feeling in my stomach. A girl who flew into the bush just to make sure Bruce was safe had to be pretty special to him, hadn't she?

Maybe she's only his sister, I tried to argue to myself. *Or a close friend he grew up with.* I had almost convinced myself of this when she got ready to go.

"No, I won't stay for a cup of tea, thank

you," she said to Kay, who had invited her to join us for lunch. Her face clearly said that we, and our table and food, were much too dirty and primitive for her. "And please don't take any more risks and make me worry about you again, Bruce," she said. She reached up to stroke his cheek, and the kiss she gave him was anything but sisterly. Then she picked her way daintily over the burned-out ground, climbed into the helicopter, and was gone.

When I was a little kid, my father took me to a fair and bought me a beautiful, heart-shaped balloon. I was so happy to have it. I carried it around all day tied to my wrist, and I couldn't wait to get home and show it to Mommy. Then, just as I was getting out of the car in front of our house, it popped. That was exactly how I felt as I watched Pamela fly away. I had just found someone I could confide in, someone to whom I could open my heart. And pop!

What a dummy you are, Tiffany, I said to myself bitterly as I picked at the last of my lunch. My appetite had suddenly gone. *Just because Bruce was nice to you last night, you let your imagination run away with you. He saw you were upset and scared,*

*and he felt sorry for you. He's a nice person.
There was nothing more to it than that.*

The others around the table were enjoying
their meal again and equally enjoying teasing
Bruce. "Only someone like Mick Dawson's son
would have his girlfriend flown in to visit
him in the outback," my father said, laughing.

"Come on, Bruce, who is she?" Adam urged.

Bruce blushed. "Oh, she's just an old friend,"
he said, drawing lines with his fork down the
tablecloth.

"Oh, sure, she looked like an old friend,"
Adam said, grinning.

"Bruce, was that Pamela Morton by any
chance?" Kay asked. "I'm sure I've seen her
in the newspapers on the society pages."

"That's right," Bruce said, still drawing lines
with his fork.

"You know Pamela Morton," Kay said to
the rest of us. "Her father owns Morton's
department stores."

Department stores, I thought gloomily. *Of
course, he'd date another rich kid!* The funny
thing was that I had really forgotten Bruce
was a millionaire's son. Now I remembered it
all too painfully. *Let's face it,* I thought. *I
haven't got a chance against a girl like that.
I never stood a chance. When he gets home*

after this trip, he won't even remember I exist.

"You're very quiet, Tiffany," my father said, "and you've hardly touched your food. Are you feeling OK?"

"I'm fine, thank you," I muttered. "But if you'll all excuse me, I'd better go pack my things."

"I hope she's all right," I heard my father saying. "I hope she didn't get too much of a shock last night. She's not used to this sort of thing."

"I don't think it was anything to do with last night that turned her off her food," Sam's gravelly voice cut in, "and I think we'd all better start loading those cars if we want to get out of here today."

Had my face given away too much? I wondered. Had Sam understood what happened the night before and that morning? I'd have to watch my behavior more carefully in the future. I didn't want people thinking I was in love with Bruce. Even if it just might be true!

Chapter Eight

We left an hour later, driving hard and leaving a trail of blackened dust behind us. We traveled almost without stopping the whole next day, too. Looking out of the Land Rover was like watching a stage after a play is over and the scenery is being removed. First, the forest went, to be replaced with grass and a few trees, like a park. Then, the grass and trees grew sparser and sparser until finally we were in a desert. The only tree growing was next to a water hole. At last I began to understand the real meaning of the word "expedition." I remembered all the dried food and water containers that had seemed so stupid in Sydney. From now on there were going to be no more koala sanctuaries, no more isolated towns with cabins or stores to shop in. We were on our own.

We had left paved roads far behind and bounced over rocky trails. "This is killing my back," Adam remarked after we had stopped for a lunch break. "I don't think that Land Rover has any springs at all. Couldn't we have driven north on a good road?" he asked my father.

"Certainly not," Dad answered, taking a gulp of water. "One of the goals of this trip is to follow the first overland trail to the north coast."

"Only, of course, the first expedition didn't make it back," Bruce said with a wicked smile.

"You're a good person to have around," Adam quipped, "a real positive thinker."

"They took camels, instead of cars," Bruce added, "so the ride was probably a bit softer for them."

"Yes, I think I'd prefer a camel with nice, soft feet," I said thoughtfully.

"They have another advantage, too," Bruce said, tossing me a peach from the cooler.

"What's that? They don't need gas?"

"No, if you run out of food in the desert, you can eat them!"

"You are gross! I bet you could never kill and eat a camel!"

"Who said anything about kill? I'd wait until it died from exhaustion, then cut a few steaks off where it lay!"

"You really are gross," I said, laughing, "but I bet you wouldn't. I think you're an old softie at heart. You'd probably have grown so fond of it that you'd dig a big grave for it."

He gave me a smile as he climbed back into the Land Rover. "You're right, I probably would," he said.

Bruce and I were getting on as well as ever. Nobody had mentioned Pamela since she disappeared into the wide blue yonder, and I certainly was not going to bring her up again. There were times when I even felt hopeful about Bruce and me, when I believed that he liked me as more than a friend. When he touched my shoulder while he told me about desert plants or grabbed my hand and asked me to come and look at a beautiful view, I could feel the electricity flowing between us. I just hoped he could, too, and that the feeling was not only on my side. Surely I was not imagining that he looked at me in a special way sometimes. At night beside the camp fire, he would choose to sit next to me, and in the darkness his hand would brush against mine.

But I had no real way of knowing whether the beginnings of this romance were only happening in my head. For one thing, we never had a chance to be alone. Out in the middle of a desert there really wasn't anywhere to go to get away from Sam or Adam, both of whom would have loved to tease us. And I didn't love the idea of having my first romance with my father watching every move. Besides, we were working so hard and the heat during the day was so horrible that none of us spoke unless absolutely necessary. So, I kept on hoping. But at night when I was so tired I felt like crying and when I tried to comb the tangles from my matted hair and put lotion on my millions of mosquito bites, I would remember the beautiful Pamela, looking as I always intended to look, waiting for Bruce at home. And then it seemed pretty hopeless.

I now slept in the back of one of the Land Rovers. I had made this monumental decision after I met a centipede, a hairy hotdog type insect, and Bruce had mentioned that it was poisonous as well as revolting looking. That settled it for me. The thought of a snake coming into my bag was bad enough, but the thought of that hairy insect coming to join me was more than I could bear!

One day we crossed a broken mountain

range full of gullies. In the middle we came across a creek, and my father allowed us a rare, unscheduled stop to get wet. I was lying back contentedly, staring up at the sky between red rocks, when Bruce came to get me.

"Come on, I've got something to show you," he said.

"Now? I was just enjoying myself for the first time in weeks."

"You'll really want to see this," he said, and he dragged me out of the water. I let him. I wasn't going to be dumb enough to miss a chance to go anywhere with Bruce, and I wondered whether he was just inventing an excuse for us to be alone. I followed him up one of those dark cracks in the rock until we came to a smooth, curved overhang.

"I thought you'd like to see these," he said, pointing at the wall. Then I noticed that the rock was decorated with red and black paintings—skeletonlike fish, stick figures of men and animals, and abstract designs.

"It's an aboriginal holy place," he said. "You can usually find them around a good water hole." He put his arm around me. "Now look up there," he said. I looked, but I was more aware that his arm was tight around my shoulder, that his cheek was touching mine.

"Bruce! Where are you?" My brother's voice

echoed among the rocks. "Get down here quick!" Then Adam appeared in person. "Come on, move it," he said, grinning. "Your friend Pamela has just come on the radio, and she wants to talk to you."

Bruce let go of my shoulder and ran back down the gully. I watched him go.

"I'd give up on him if I were you," Adam said kindly as we walked back together. "You're not going to win against a girl like Pamela."

"What do you mean?" I asked, glad that my face was already so sunburned that a blush couldn't make any difference.

"Oh, come on. I'm not blind, you know," Adam said. "You follow him around like a baby kangaroo ready for a feeding."

"I do not!" I said hotly.

"Well, your eyes do," he said and smiled. "Forget it, kid. Millionaires tend to stick together, you know. You don't have a chance."

I could feel Bruce's cheek against mine. *Just a slight chance,* I thought, *just a slight one.*

When we got back to the vehicles, Bruce's radio call was already over. After what Adam had said, I tried not to look at him. Was it so obvious to everyone that I followed him around? I made myself climb into the Land

Rover, open my purse, and sit brushing my hair as if Bruce Dawson were the last thing on my mind. But I did manage to sneak one small peek at him as he got into the driver's seat. He didn't look very pleased, not at all like someone who'd just spoken to the love of his life. When Adam made a joke about Pamela checking up to make sure he was behaving himself, Bruce snapped back and told him to lay off the cheap jokes. Bruce was normally the most easygoing guy. He loved to tease and be teased, and so I guessed that something was pretty wrong.

His bad temper continued all that day. He drove, staring straight ahead and not speaking. Sometimes I caught a glimpse of his face in the mirror. He was frowning. What had Pamela said that made him so mad? Had she told him that she was going with someone else? In that case, there might be a chance for me. Had he told her that he liked me now? No, that was too much to hope for. And it wouldn't make him look angry. I wished I had the nerve to ask him what was wrong. He had helped me so much when I was upset, maybe I could do the same for him. But I remembered how he had snapped at Adam, and so I kept quiet.

In the middle of the night, we passed from

dry to wet. We had decided to drive through the night from then on because the days were becoming unbearably hot. Around midnight I had dozed off uncomfortably with my head against a case of film. I had gone to sleep with the crisp cold of the desert night raising goose bumps on my arms. But when I opened my eyes a little while later, I sensed immediately that something was different. For a moment I couldn't think what. Then I realized the air was no longer crisp and cool: it was warm and sticky. I had thought that desert heat was unbearable, but this was much worse. I felt as if I couldn't even breathe. My clothes were sticking to me, wet with perspiration. Just before dawn a fine rain began to fall. It was as warm as driving through a shower. Day broke to heavy, lead-colored clouds and a landscape of mud. There were a few large pools of water, around which flocks of birds gathered.

"With this sort of weather, we must be getting close to the gulf," Adam said as we lurched through the mud.

"Not that close," Bruce said, fighting to keep the Land Rover on what was left of the trail. "Normally this area is desert, too. Cyclone Angela is sitting off Queensland and blowing in all this wet air."

"That Angela sure is making trouble," Adam remarked.

"She's not the only girl doing that," Bruce said. He didn't even smile when he said this.

It rained steadily all day. At times the entire plain was under inches of water so that it looked as if we were driving across an ocean. Mosquitoes followed us, humming happily every time we slowed down, which we did often since the road had become treacherous.

"Where are we planning to spend the night, Dad?" Adam called when the two vehicles slowed to cross a creek. The creek was filled with muddy, brown water that swirled past us dangerously fast. Sam went ahead, wading to test it, and came back saying that it was safe to cross.

"There's no station closer than Faversham," Bruce remarked, looking up from the map.

"I was planning to camp out one more night," my father said, looking worried. "We can't make that drive in less than a day, and I don't want to drive through the darkness with floods like these. But now I'm not sure that we can find a place that's safe to camp."

I stared out across the total flatness. Not a tree in sight. Giant termite mounds or anthills, taller than men, were the only things breaking the horizon, and they looked very much like gravestones. I brushed a dozen or so mosquitoes from my face and wished, for an instant, that I was back in New York. Then I pushed the thought away. This was one of those bad times. The good times made it all worthwhile.

"There's one bit of higher ground beyond Bonner's Creek," Sam said, peering out across the floods. "Maybe we should try and spend the night there. I think there are even a couple of trees there, if I remember right. This is an odd situation. Floods in December, who ever heard of it!"

"See if you can get the people at Faversham on the radio, Adam," Dad said. "At least let them know we're coming."

After a lot of crackle, Adam managed to get through, but the call wasn't much help. The owners of the cattle station, or ranch, were up on the northern part of their property with all their trucks, and their young son was alone in the house. He said his parents were trying to round up cattle caught in the floods and he didn't know when they'd be back. He told us to call again after we'd crossed Bonner's Creek.

So we set off again, slithering and lurching as the wheels tried to grip the mud. Until then I had just been annoyed and bored. Now

I really began to feel scared. The water stretched out on all sides of us in a giant muddy sheet. What's more, with the constant rain it was getting deeper all the time. What if the Land Rover really got stuck and the water rose? There'd be nobody to rescue us. I had this horrible vision of trying to swim through that muddy water, not knowing which direction to swim in, getting more and more tired, meeting snakes and bugs and . . .

"Look, there's a crocodile!" Adam yelled. Something long and brown slithered away and disappeared into the water with almost no splash. The others all seemed excited about seeing it and kept looking for others. My father even got out his camera, ready to take pictures. I can't say that I felt very excited about it at all. Terrified, maybe, but not excited.

Just as the daylight was beginning to fade, we saw ahead of us one lone tree with a little rise of dry land under it.

"There it is," Sam called back to us. "That's the tree I was thinking of, and there's Bonner's Creek."

Bonner's Creek didn't look too inviting. It was visible only as a fast-moving current in the stretch of endless flood. Muddy water swirled around trapped branches and passed with a roar.

"Do you think we can make it across tonight, Sam?" my father asked, looking anxiously at the fast-flowing water.

Sam scratched his head and pushed back his old hat, something he always did when he was thinking. "Listen, mate, it's going to be worse tomorrow," he said at last. "I reckon if we don't get across tonight, we ain't ever going to get past this flamin' creek. Tell you what, I'll try it out a bit and see where it's possible." Then he started toward the swirling water.

"Don't be crazy, Sam," my brother called after him. "You'll be swept away."

Sam turned back and grinned. "Listen, mate, I've crossed enough of these things in my life to know which ones are likely to sweep me away. Besides, I know how to swim."

I found myself holding my breath as he walked down into the creek. It lapped around his knees to start with, then his thighs. Surely a Land Rover couldn't make it through that. He reached the far bank and turned to come back to us. He had almost made it back and was already grinning when his feet were swept from under him and he was snatched into the water as easily as a fallen leaf. We rushed to the creek's edge, then ran along the bank, but it was useless. The water was carrying him so fast and the bank was so waterlogged that we just couldn't keep up with him. We saw the terrifying sight of his hat disappearing farther and farther down the stream. How long could he keep his head above water? He was pretty old, after all.

"Sam!" I heard myself yelling as I dashed along the bank. "Hang on, Sam." I remembered that I hadn't liked him initially and felt guilty about it.

"What's all the flamin' row about?" came a voice below us, and there was Sam wedged against a large tree limb in the stream. The boys waded in and dragged him out. He didn't seem the least bit scared or upset, only a little annoyed that he had had to be rescued. "I would have gotten out just fine on my own if people had minded their own business," he complained. "That ain't the first creek I ever fell in. I'm used to it, there's nothing to it. You just let yourself go with the water until you bump up against something to hang on to." He stomped back to the cars. "OK. Take them across," he said. "The bottom's fairly solid."

We went first, with Bruce driving. I could feel the water pushing the Land Rover around, and it came right over the low side of the vehicle and onto the floor of the car. It was surprisingly cold on our feet. But the engine kept running smoothly, and it didn't take long before we were climbing the far bank and were safe on that dry little hill under the twisted gum tree.

Then my father's Land Rover went across. We watched as it crept toward us like a large water beetle. Suddenly it lurched, and there was a horrible crunching sound, like metal breaking. The engine stopped.

"What happened, Dad?" Adam yelled.

"I must have hit a rock," my father called back. "Looks like we broke the oil pan." A film of oil was already floating around the car and drifting away with the current. "Give me the rope and you can tow us in," Dad called.

It seemed to take hours to find the rope, throw it to them, and attach it to their car. We started our engine. It whined and groaned, protesting, and neither car budged. It wasn't any good. Dad's Land Rover was stuck solidly in the muddy bottom, and we were just not strong enough to pull it out. What's more, the water was clearly rising. Even as we watched, it splashed over the open back of the Land Rover. We formed a human chain to pass up anything that could be lifted, and soon we had our belongings piled around us on the island, looking just like the Swiss Family Robinson.

"Well, at least we got the cameras out safely," my father said.

"And the food," Adam agreed, showing clearly what was dearest to each of their hearts.

"I've just thought of something," Bruce said suddenly. "The radio's in that car."

We all stared down at the half-submerged vehicle. I wondered if everyone else was experiencing the same sinking feeling that I was. We were stranded on a little patch of land a few yards wide, and we had no way of letting anyone know where we were!

Chapter Nine

We spent that night huddled together under the tree. We tried lighting a fire to cook on, but it rained harder and harder so that even Sam couldn't get one going. We munched on cold food while the rain found holes to drip through the tarpaulin we had rigged over our heads. It was definitely not the best night of my life. I can tell you just how bad I was feeling. I was sitting next to Bruce and didn't even notice it! As it got darker, my thoughts got gloomier and gloomier. I imagined the water rising to cover the island. I imagined us climbing into the scrawny little tree while the crocodiles swam around below, waiting for one of us to fall asleep and drop down to them. Then I realized that there was nothing to stop a crocodile from climbing up onto the little patch of dry land right then. That made me decide that I definitely, but definitely, would not fall asleep that night.

But I suppose I must have fallen asleep in the end because I had a very weird dream. I dreamed I was outside my house in Westchester. I remember standing outside our front door and thinking, *Thank heavens it's all over. Now I can get clean and dry and go to sleep in my own bed.* But when my mother opened the door, she took one look at me and screamed.

"Tiffany, what have you done to yourself! You look just terrible. Your clothes are all dirty, your hair is a mess. You are not coming in here looking like that!"

"But, Mom, please let me in. I'm tired and wet, and I want to come home," I begged.

"Then go and clean yourself up first," she said coldly. "You are not bringing mud onto my white carpet."

Then I was in a river, trying to scrub myself clean enough so that I could go home. But the river was muddy, and however hard I tried, I put more mud on than I took off. So I went from house to house, begging people to let me use their bathrooms. At last I was clean, and I ran back to my front door. But when I got there, I found a note on it saying, "Not at home. Gone away with Felix."

Then I saw my father driving down the street in a Land Rover. I called out to him and he stopped, but he looked at me as if he didn't know me. "You can't come with us," he said. "You're much too clean." Then he drove away, leaving me alone on the sidewalk.

"Come back," I yelled after him. "Don't leave me alone!"

I must have yelled out loud because I felt a hand on my arm. "Hey, Tiffany, relax, it's all right," Bruce said quietly.

I sat up, feeling embarrassed. "Did I wake you up?"

"No, I couldn't sleep," he said. "What's the matter? Did you have a bad dream?"

"I guess so," I said. "I was back in New York, and my mother wouldn't take me in because I was covered in mud. Dumb, huh? I don't know why I got so upset because I'm not even sure if I want to live with her anymore. Especially now that she's got Felix— that's my new stepfather. I've been thinking about it a lot while we've been driving. And the more I think, the less I seem to belong in her sort of world anymore."

"Would you live with your father, then?" Bruce asked.

"I don't know," I said. "I'm not even sure he'd want me. In my dream he just drove off and left me. It was pretty scary."

"I guess we're all feeling a bit scared," Bruce said. "I can tell you, I don't like the feeling of being trapped on this little piece of land."

"Me, neither," I agreed.

"I'm sure we can't be far from that station," Bruce said. "I feel like going for help."

"In the Land Rover, you mean?"

"No, on foot. We don't want to risk getting it stuck in the mud, too. Besides, the water's not that deep. I've got to do something. You want to come?"

"But how would we know the way?" I asked nervously. I was torn between wanting to be with Bruce and not wanting to get lost forever in the middle of nowhere.

"I thought I saw a line of trees before it got dark," he said, "and we do have a good compass. All we have to do is keep walking north, and we'll come to the station boundary."

"Do you think my father would let us?" I whispered, looking across at his sleeping form huddled under the tarp.

"We'll leave him a note," Bruce said. "He'll be pleased when we bring help. If we just sit here, nobody is going to know where we are."

"Well, OK," I said hesitantly. "When do you want to start?"

"It's getting light right now," he said. "Let's get going before anyone else wakes up. I don't feel like doing a lot of arguing about whether or not it's safe to go."

He tiptoed over the sleeping people, grabbed my backpack, and dumped the clothes out. My makeup, by the way, had been lost somewhere a week before, and I was just as happy not to lug it around. Bruce stuffed some dried fruit and beef jerky into the pack, then took the compass from the Land Rover.

"OK, partner, let's get going," he said with a grin. He held out his hand to me. I looked back quickly to see if my father was waking up yet, then I reached out to take Bruce's hand. It felt warm and reassuring, and I think I would have followed him almost anywhere at that moment.

Hiking really wasn't too bad. Most of the time the water was only a few inches deep, and we didn't sink too far into the mud. There were patches where our shoes got stuck and came out with huge plops, but all that was kind of fun with Bruce. He hadn't said anything about what had made him so angry two days before, but it obviously wasn't bothering him anymore. Now he was like a little boy having great fun doing something not allowed.

After a couple of hours, we stopped for a rest, perching on top of a hill to eat a few bites of food. We could see the line of trees from the ranch quite clearly now, and that made us hopeful. We started hiking once again, giggling and teasing each other every time one of us stumbled. We got more and more caked with mud until we looked like two swamp creatures. I had forgotten about the dangers we could meet until suddenly I saw a long, brown shape gliding toward us.

"Bruce!" I yelled, "there's a crocodile. Quick, let's run to that giant anthill."

Instead of running, Bruce started laughing. "You city girls are scared of your own shadows," he said.

"Well, you might enjoy having your leg bitten off, but don't expect me to carry you afterward," I said, hurrying to the anthill and scrambling clear of the water.

"One of the basic lessons of survival," Bruce said calmly, "is to recognize the difference between a crocodile and a log." Then he bent down and grabbed the floating log for me to examine.

"Very funny," I said, stomping on ahead of him. "It looked like a crocodile to me."

But he continued to tease me about it as we walked. "Watch out for man-eating logs," he kept calling until I was so mad at him I wished I hadn't come.

"I don't know why I ever thought you were cute," I snapped, then instantly regretted it. He looked at me with interest.

"I didn't know you *did* think I was cute," he said with an adorable little smile. "I mean, we had fun for a while, but then the day before yesterday you started being very cool again. I thought you hated me."

"I'd hardly come on a crazy trip like this with someone I hated," I said, striding ahead of him.

He hurried after me and grabbed my shoulder, turning me toward him. "So I'm cute, huh?"

"You'll have to ask Pamela that," I said, trying to break free from him.

"I know what Pamela thinks," he said, "but I want to know how you feel."

"Why? Is it so good for your ego to know that every girl adores you?" I asked.

"Only certain girls," he said. "Do you realize that I've been trying to get you alone for this whole trip, and there's always been someone to interrupt us? Well, we now have several miles of outback between us and the nearest person."

"Was there anything special you wanted to tell me when we were alone?" I asked in a voice hardly louder than a whisper.

"Only this," he said. His fingers gently took my chin and brought my face toward his, then his lips met mine in a sweet, melting kiss. He looked down at me, his eyes searching mine as if he weren't sure I wanted him to go on.

"Well, this time no one is going to interrupt us," I said, my eyes smiling up at him. Suddenly there was no past nor future, nobody else in the world, no complications in either of our lives. I was there, and he was beside me. This was the moment I had been waiting for. His arms came around me. He hugged me against his chest as his lips sought mine. But before we could kiss, he jumped back with a cry of alarm.

"What is it?" I yelled. His face was white with fear.

"I think I've just been bitten by a snake," he said. "Let me hold on to you a second." He leaned against my shoulder and lifted his foot clear of the water.

As soon as I saw it, I started to laugh. "A snake, eh?" I asked. "You city boys can't tell

the difference between a snake and a crayfish."
The large crayfish that had been pinching
his ankle let go and fell back into the water
with a plop.

"It felt like a snake," he said, frowning at
me. "It hurt as much as a snake."

"Poor baby," I said teasingly. "Do you want
me to kiss it and make it all better?"

"Just wait until I get you on dry land," he
said, starting to laugh.

"I'd say that makes us even, wouldn't you?"
I asked, my eyes laughing triumphantly into
his.

"Very even," he whispered. "In fact, just
right for each other." And he took me into
his arms again.

"You know what happened the last time
you tried to kiss me," I warned. "This time it
might be a real snake. I think we ought to
keep going. I don't want to spend a night out
here, even if it is with you."

"Wise girl," he said. "OK, lead on. I'll just
limp behind dragging my wounded ankle."
We set off again, giggling like a couple of
two-year-olds.

By about midafternoon those trees were still
in front of us, but they didn't look any nearer.
"Do you think we really will make it before it
gets dark?" I asked.

"Don't worry. Even if we don't, we'll just choose a large termite mound and spend the night there."

"Just the night I've always dreamed of," I said dryly. "You and three million termites."

"Let's rest a couple of minutes on that huge one over there," he said. "In spite of the cruel way you laughed about my injury, that crayfish did make my ankle bleed. I'd better check on the wound."

I was glad to rest, too. We scrambled to the top of an anthill and perched together side by side. "Look, you can even see the house from up here," Bruce said. "We'll be safely on dry land in an hour or two."

I started feeling much better as soon as I saw the buildings. "I can't believe it," I said. "We'll be sleeping in real beds tonight. We'll have real food to eat, no mosquitoes, no—"

"What's that noise?" Bruce asked suddenly.

"It sounds like some sort of engine." I strained my ears to hear the distant putt-putt. "Do you think they're sending out a boat for us?"

"Oh, no," Bruce said, frowning as he looked up. "I have a horrible suspicion of what it is."

A few seconds later, a helicopter came into view and swept low toward us. It hovered overhead, its noise deafening, its blades whipping everything into a frenzy around us. When it was only a few feet above us, a door opened, and a ladder was lowered. From the open doorway, Pamela's perfect face peered down.

"Darling, we've been worried sick about you," she called. "They're sending out trucks, but I wanted to be the one who found you first!"

Bruce looked up at her and frowned. "Go away," he called. "We don't want to be rescued!"

Chapter Ten

We sat together on top of the giant anthill while the helicopter rose into the sky, then swooped away like a giant bird. As it disappeared into the distance, we looked at each other and burst out laughing. "Do you know what you've done?" I asked Bruce when I had stopped laughing enough to talk. "Now we might never be rescued."

"I can think of worse fates," he said, giving me a long, delicious look that turned me instantly to jelly.

"Much as I think being stranded with you would not be bad at all," I said, "I don't think a chunk of mud two feet square is much basis for a long and happy life."

He laughed again, so loudly that several large birds rose up out of the water and flapped away. "Have I ever told you that you're adorable?" he said, stroking my chin with his finger. "And that you have the most incredible blue eyes and cute little nose?"

"No, you haven't," I said, "but you can tell me now if you like."

"Very well," he said seriously. "You're adorable, and you have the most incredible blue eyes and cute little nose." Then he leaned forward and gave my nose a tiny, gentle kiss. I couldn't help remembering the times I had scowled at myself in the mirror, wishing that my nose weren't so little-girlish and that my face would start looking more like a fashion model's. Now I wouldn't have traded it for anything in the world. If Bruce liked it, that was good enough for me! I didn't want to look like Pamela at all anymore.

Pamela! The realization of what Bruce had just done hit me all at once. "You told Pamela to go away!" I said. He nodded, looking at me calmly and with that hint of amusement that had annoyed me so much at first. "She won't like that very much," I said.

He nodded again. "She will absolutely hate it," he agreed.

"Does that mean it's all over between you two?" I hardly dared ask.

"Looks like it," he said.

"Oh." I didn't dare say another word on the subject. It was too good to be true, and I didn't want to ruin things. We sat for a few minutes in silence. "Do you think we should walk on?" I asked. "I have a procession of ants marching over my right foot."

"No, don't go," he said, putting a hand on my arm. "I don't want to go back to having other people around us, not yet. I want to explain about Pamela and me."

"You don't have to," I said. "I mean, it's none of my business—"

"It's not the way you think," he said. "I was just going through it in my own mind so that I could explain it properly to you. You see, Pamela really means nothing to me—"

"Oh, sure," I said. "A girl follows some guy in a helicopter, and he means nothing to her."

"I didn't say I meant nothing to her," he said. "It's the other way around."

"I don't quite follow you," I said. "Are you telling me that the romance was all one-sided?"

"Well, not exactly," he said, wrinkling his nose as if he were a bit embarrassed. "After all, she *is* a great-looking girl, and she's very warm and—"

"You don't have to go on," I said quickly. "I get the picture."

He grinned. "We grew up together." He stared out across the flooded landscape. "Our families are close friends, and so at every party it was 'Bruce and Pamela, don't they make a lovely couple.' I didn't mind going to parties and things with her, but then she started to get serious. In a way, it's almost silly. I mean she and I are completely different. She likes all the things I hate. Just look at how important clothes and makeup are to her. Pamela thinks a day in the wilderness means spending a few hours sunbathing on her parents' lawn. It would never have worked, but she didn't understand that. You see, Pamela is very spoiled, and she's used to getting her own way. She just was not going to accept that she wasn't going to get me!"

"She certainly tries hard," I said. "I don't think I'd have the nerve to chase someone in a helicopter."

"That's because you're not like her," Bruce said. "At first I thought you were. But then I saw that deep down you care about things that really matter. You don't put yourself first all the time the way Pamela does. And you have the cutest little nose."

"Shut up about my nose," I said, laughing. "You'll give me a complex. But do you honestly think Pamela will quit trying now that she's seen you happily on your own anthill with me?"

"I doubt it," he said. "Pamela is not a quitter. She really wants me to come home. She even tried to get my family to bring me back. That call the other day—I was so angry."

"Yes, I noticed," I said.

"Pamela had talked to my mother and got her very worried about me. My father came on the radio and said he wanted me home for Christmas because my mother was making herself sick fretting about me. I said I wasn't coming. We had a big shouting match. The thing that makes me mad is that my mother isn't the type to get nervous without good reason. She probably never would have thought about having me home for Christmas if Pamela hadn't told her stories about what terrible danger I was in."

"Christmas!" I said, shaking my head in disbelief. "I can't believe it's almost Christmas."

"Only a few more days," Bruce said.

"It hardly seems possible," I said. "To think they probably have snow in New York. Everyone's shopping for presents, the store windows are all lit up—"

"Do you wish you were home?" he asked.

"No. I'd rather spend Christmas this year

with a line of ants crawling up my leg. What about you? Do you have to go?"

"I'm not going to," he said. "I'm seventeen now. I'm not a little boy. I don't have to go running home just because my parents want me to. You know, Tiff, it's very hard growing up with a father like mine. He started out with nothing but a few acres of land and a couple hundred sheep. From that, he built the most successful sheep business in all of Australia. He knows what he wants, and he makes sure he gets it. Most of the time I just go along with him because it's the easiest thing to do. But I'm beginning to stand up for myself. It's not just this trip. You see, I want to go to college, and Dad doesn't think it's necessary. Actually, I applied without telling him. I have no idea what he'll say when he finds out. But I can't go on doing things his way just because I'm afraid to face him. I decided the other day that I've got to make him realize I'm my own person, too."

"Good for you," I said. "I think we've both come a long way on this trip."

"And I think we're just about to go a little farther," Bruce said, peering out toward the horizon. "Looks like they're sending out a truck for us."

*　　*　　*

Half an hour later we were bumping and lurching toward the station house. "So what happened to the young lady in the helicopter?" the owner yelled to us above the noise of the engine. "She said she was going to pick you up, then she radios back here and says she's not going to after all."

"I think she decided to go home," Bruce yelled back and squeezed my hand.

"Who was she, anyway? Not the regular rescue service!"

"No, not the regular rescue service," Bruce said. "A sort of private bodyguard, only I didn't need it."

I was flabbergasted when I stepped into the house. A big, realistic-looking Christmas tree reached to the ceiling in one corner; it was covered in glass balls and twinkling lights, and white powder was sprinkled on the branches to look like snow. It was like stepping out of a time machine. One minute we were sitting in the steamy heat watching ants crawl over us, brushing away mosquitoes and staring at empty miles of flooded fields. The next minute we were in the middle of a scene straight off a Christmas card. It hardly seemed possible.

One not so pleasant surprise was my father. He walked over to me, and, boy, did he look furious. "Do you realize what an irresponsible thing you did this morning!" he barked. "If you had made the least little mistake in direction, you would have been lost forever out there. Furthermore, one of us might have gone to search for you and become lost, too. You cannot take risks in this sort of country. Now, I'm in charge, I give the orders!"

"It was entirely my fault, sir," Bruce said, stepping forward to stand between Dad and me. "I didn't like waiting to be rescued, and I could see the line of trees around the house clearly, and so I was sure of the direction."

My father sighed. "Can you imagine me trying to explain to your father if anything happened to you?"

"What could have happened?" Bruce said. "I could see where I was heading, the water was only ankle deep most of the time, and there were plenty of anthills to rest on, weren't there, Tiff?"

"I'm even more amazed that you went, Tiffany," my father said. "The same girl who was scared of my dog and of insects crawling into her sleeping bag. You didn't even want to come at all. And suddenly you're not scared to walk through snake- and crocodile-infested floods. It doesn't make sense to me."

"Bruce needed some company," I said, trying to keep myself from smiling.

"So if I ask you to come scuba diving for sharks because I need some company, you'll come?" my father snapped.

"Don't be dumb, Dad," Adam chimed in. "She wouldn't go with you, you're not Bruce."

The light suddenly dawned on my father. "Oh," he said slowly. "It's like that, is it? Well, you two lovebirds, stay where I can keep an eye on you in future."

"I think it was for just that reason that they slipped away," Adam said, grinning. He turned to us. "Maybe I should mention that there's a terrific sunset out there right now. It would be a shame to waste it!"

"Good idea, mate," Bruce said, winking at Adam. "I don't think we ought to waste a sunset, do you, Tiff?" Before I could say anything, Bruce took my hand and led me outside.

"Let's walk a little," he said.

Together we strolled past the outbuildings until we stood at the edge of the floodwater and looked out across a magical landscape. Beneath the bank of heavy clouds, the sky had cleared and the world was flooded with light. Steaks of red, pink, and orange danced across the water and tinted the clouds above.

"A perfect ending to a perfect day," Bruce said. Then he took me in his arms and kissed me. This time, there were no suspected snakes to interrupt us. We were alone, with all the time in the world, and that kiss seemed to last forever. When we finally looked up, we saw that we had company. Hundreds of tiny birds had come down to the edge of the water, the pink parrots and bright green parakeets I had seen earlier in the expedition. They chattered noisily to one another as they took drinks.

"You know what we call them in Australia, don't you?" Bruce asked me. "Lovebirds. That's a good sign for us, don't you think?"

"You bet," I said, snuggling close to him, feeling warm in his strong arms. Then I said seriously, "I try not to think about the future because we have so few days left together. For the first time in my whole life, I've met a boy who really understands me, but in two weeks I'll be leaving again. It doesn't seem fair."

"Don't worry about it," Bruce said, stroking my hair. "Two weeks are a long time. And things have a way of working themselves out if you wish hard enough."

The sun flamed brilliantly red, and we watched as its last rays dropped below the horizon. "We ought to go inside, I guess," I whispered to Bruce.

"I suppose we should," he said.

We walked back slowly, our arms around each other, not speaking.

Chapter Eleven

The Barbers made us feel very welcome at their home and begged us to stay with them for the holidays. "We'd welcome the company," Mrs. Barber insisted, "and you folks look like you could do with a good rest."

I looked across at my father, hoping he'd say yes. Then we'd have a real Christmas dinner and be able to sleep in beds for a few nights longer. And Bruce and I could find a few more sunsets to watch.

But my father shook his head. "Thanks very much, but I'm afraid we have to push on," he said. "We really appreciate your help in getting the Land Rover out and fixed and in looking after us so generously, but we have a date in a couple of days with a man who hunts crocodiles."

131

"I don't mind staying on here with Bruce while you go and film your crocodiles," I said hopefully.

My father laughed. "Nothing doing, kid. You said once before that you'd rather stay at the hotel than come on the expedition, right? You'll love the crocs. And besides, we aren't coming back this way. After the crocodiles we swing east toward the ocean and then down the coast to Sydney."

"I could always ask Pamela to pop back in her helicopter," Bruce said, and he winked at me.

"She'd give you a ride all right, but she'd probably push me out over the desert," I said, laughing. I turned to my father. "OK, I give in, although I can think of a million better ways to spend Christmas than watch someone hunt crocodiles."

"What about watching Mom and Felix hunt for a good restaurant to have Christmas dinner in?" Adam asked.

"I'd much prefer the crocodiles," I agreed. "All right, let's get going."

So we spent Christmas Day in the sweltering heat beside a muddy river watching my father rush up and down the bank madly filming crocodiles. He seemed very pleased at the end of the day and said he had gotten some marvelous footage. I couldn't say whether that was true or not because I wasn't standing close enough to judge. However brave and fearless I had become, I was not fool enough to be standing right in the escape route of a frightened or angry crocodile!

In the evening we all celebrated with a good meal. I had definitely had enough of Sam's cooking, which never changed from day to day. I decided to take over the camping stove and make something, if not fantastic, at least different. I used most of the provisions the Barbers had given us and made a terrific stew and gooey fruit dessert. The others appreciated it, and Sam said I was turning into a regular little swagman's sheila—which I think was a compliment, but I wasn't sure!

After that we didn't get many more good meals until we hit the coast, several hundred miles across wet, hot, empty country. I got skilled at coaxing Land Rovers through flooded creeks and finding the way strictly by compass and radio when it was too dark to see the trail. In fact, just when I was really becoming able to handle myself in the wilderness, we drove into the little town of Cairns. There was the Coral Sea, gleaming in front of us. We passed a scattering of stores. It was funny to remember that a few weeks before, I would have thought a town like Cairns hopelessly backward and primitive. I would have laughed at the old-fashioned stores and the women in their cotton dresses and ankle socks. But now it looked as built up as New York or Hollywood. We all made ourselves sick on the comforts of civilization, like hamburgers and ice cream. Then it was back to work again, driving down the coast photographing sharks.

We had been so busy that Bruce and I had had hardly any time to be alone. I treasured the memory of that romantic sunset at the Barbers'. I didn't even have time to think about leaving Bruce and going back to Westchester and Mom. It was when we arrived at Bruce's house at the end of our trip that the future finally hit me in the face.

As we pulled up in front of the Dawsons' house outside Sydney, Bruce asked me, "What do you think of it?"

We were planning to stay for a few days before we flew back to California, and from there, I'd fly back to New York. I guess I must have looked surprised because Bruce laughed. "Everyone reacts that way when they see the house for the first time. But we like it."

"It's not that I don't like it," I said quickly, "it's just that I wasn't expecting it to look this way."

"I know what you mean," he said and covered my hand with his. That was one of the wonderful things about Bruce. He really did understand what I was feeling. "Come on, let's go and meet my mum and sisters," he said, springing out of the car ahead of me.

As I climbed out, a young kangaroo hopped across the rather moth-eaten lawn. Two big dogs chased after it barking. The kangaroo turned to face them, gave a playful kick, and bounded off again. It was clear they were old friends.

I stared at the house in wonder. It wasn't at all what I'd pictured! I mean, I had seen millionaires' houses in Beverly Hills, and they all had things like heart-shaped swimming pools and fountains. Bruce's house was big all right, but it was a shambles. The old house was almost covered with bright, creeping plants. It had large gardens, too, but they weren't orderly flower beds. Plants just grew wherever they happened to come up. The house was perched on the edge of the bush, a thick, tangled jungle that dropped dramatically into a ravine. From the front steps, you could also see the glint of white sand and the sparkle of the ocean. It felt as remote as some of the places on our trip, and yet it was only thirty minutes from downtown Sydney.

"That's what my dad likes about it so much," Bruce said. "He feels that he's right out in the bush, and yet he can get to his office quite quickly."

The front door had opened, and another huge dog bounded out, barking hysterically and trying to lick all of Bruce at once. The dog was followed by a pretty, tanned woman who looked just like Bruce, obviously his mother.

"You look marvelous," she said, hugging her son. "I was expecting you to come back all skin and bones from what Pamela was saying."

"She's just jealous, Mum," Bruce said, giving her a big smile.

"Oh, dear," his mother said, then laughed. "I should have guessed as much. Now, how about an introduction." Her gaze swept around the group and fell on me. "This can't be the young lady," she said, looking puzzled.

"There aren't any others around," Bruce said. "Mum, this is Tiffany. Tiff, this is my mother."

"Well, I'm pleased to meet you," Mrs. Dawson said, reaching out her hand to me, "and do forgive my surprised look. Pamela said you were a big, beefy outdoor girl, and I was expecting something like a female King Kong. But you're just a delicate little thing."

"Don't you believe it, Mum. There's nothing delicate about Tiffany," Bruce said, putting his arm firmly around my shoulders. "I don't know what else Pamela told you, but I'm sure it isn't true."

"You mean you weren't stranded together on top of an anthill?"

"That part was true," Bruce said and laughed. "I'll fill you in on all the details later. But right now we're all starving. Let's get something to eat."

I had really looked forward to those days at the Dawsons' with nothing to do except be with Bruce, relax, and dress up a little. During the last miles, as I sat cramped in the back of the Land Rover with one of Dad's cameras hitting me in the back of the neck every time we swung around a corner, I thought to myself, *Only four more days, then we'll be at Bruce's house!* It became a magic countdown, as I used to do before my birthday when I was a little kid.

But now that I was finally at Bruce's house, things weren't as I had imagined them at all! Oh, it was true I could have put on better clothes and done my hair beautifully. But somehow, those things didn't seem important to me anymore. Besides which, nobody in the house even noticed how anyone else was dressed. Bruce's father went to his office in shorts and sat down to dinner in a T-shirt. His mother and sisters wore shorts or faded cotton dresses. If I had spent hours making myself look great, it would have seemed as if I were trying to show off. So I stuck with the heavy hiking shorts, and Bruce and I spent the days exploring the bush. It was a lot of fun, but one thing was bothering me—the future.

One day I was sitting in a garden chair, in the shade of a large jacaranda tree, pretending to read a book, when Bruce crept up behind me. "Penny for your thoughts," he said, squatting down beside me.

"Oh, I was just reading," I said.

"No, you weren't," he said and smiled. "I've been watching you for fifteen minutes, and you haven't turned a page. So you must have other things on your mind. Want to share them?"

I heaved a big, heavy sigh. "I don't know, Bruce. It's just that we only have a few more days before I go home, and then it'll be so long before I see you. I'll miss you so much. And I've got to go back and live with my mother."

"But don't you like your mother?"

"Of course I like her, but I'm beginning to feel that I might not want to live with her. I've been thinking about this since early in the expedition. I've changed a lot, and I realize that the way she lives isn't for me now. You saw what I was like when I first arrived—"

"A bit of a pain," he said, grinning. "You looked like you'd rather miss all the excitement than get a spot on your clothes."

I grinned, too. "You're right, I really was living in an artificial world. Things are different now, and I don't want to go back to that old way of doing things."

"Can't you live with your father instead?" Bruce asked.

I shrugged my shoulders. "I don't even know if he'd want me. He and Adam get along pretty well together. And besides, my mother would be really hurt. She'd feel as if I liked my father better than I liked her."

"It does sound like a problem," Bruce agreed. We sat together in silence. A bellbird started chiming from the ravine. A gentle breeze sighed through the trees. It was almost impossible to imagine that in a week I'd be battling my way to school through the snowdrifts in Westchester. Back to Marcia and the others, back to Greg. I hadn't even thought of the gang for ages. I couldn't even picture Greg's face clearly. I realized now they had all been acquaintances, not friends. I knew it didn't really matter if I never saw them again. Since the divorce, there was only one person I had dared to trust enough to open up to. And soon I would be losing him forever. . . .

I turned to Bruce sadly. "I'm going to miss you so much."

He put his hand on my arm. "Hey, don't look like that, Tiff," he said. "It's not the end of the world. Who knows what will happen? Things may turn out just fine."

"Sure," I said bleakly. "I'll go back to Lincoln High and my mother and Felix, and you'll go back to Pamela."

"One thing I will never do," he said very firmly, "is go back to Pamela."

"Even so, you'll soon forget about me," I said. "One day, I'll show my dad's old movies to my grandchildren and say, 'That was a young man who was rather special to your grandmother once upon a time.' "

Bruce laughed and squeezed my arm. "You still have the cutest little nose," he said. "I know I'm not going to find another one like it in all of Australia. But seriously, Tiff. If you think you're the only one who has problems, you're wrong. You should try living with my father. I told you before that I applied to college against his wishes. I have no idea, though, how to tell my father."

"I can't understand a father not wanting his son to go to college," I said.

"Dad's used to doing exactly what he wants, and what he wants is for me to take over the business from him one day."

"You don't want to do that?" I asked.

He shook his head savagely. "Can you see me behind a desk, making deals to buy and sell wool?" he asked. "That's not what I want from life at all. We have some of the most beautiful wildlife in the world here in Australia. I want to go to college and learn the best way to preserve it."

"But I thought your father was really interested in preserving wildlife," I said. "Won't he let you study it?"

"He's all for it, now that he's made his millions. But he believes I should learn how to make money first, then play at preserving wildlife later. I'd go crazy with boredom!"

"Poor Bruce," I said. "What do you think he'd do if you just told him you were going to college, and that was that?"

"Whatever he'd do, it wouldn't be pleasant."

"You ought to try to make him understand your point of view," I said. "Nobody should have to spend their life living someone else's dreams for them."

"I'll try all right," Bruce said, "but he's a very stubborn man."

Chapter Twelve

Depressing as it was, my conversation with Bruce got me acting, rather than sitting around worrying. That night I nervously dialed my home phone number. An international call would be expensive, but I knew I had to straighten things out with my mother fast.

The phone rang three times before Mom picked it up. "Hello?" I said timidly.

"Tiffany, darling," my mother screamed. "We just got back from the cruise yesterday. It was lovely. Now tell me everything. I've been worried stiff about my baby way over there in Australia."

"There was nothing to worry about. I was in capable hands."

"Oh, I know your father is quite capable, but—"

"I meant my own hands, Mom," I interrupted. Then I told her a little about the expedition.

"You poor darling," Mom said when I finished. "To think of that dreadful trip in a Land Rover. If I had known your father would put you through something like that, I'd never have gone on the cruise. It makes me shudder just to think about it. No water to wash in and the insects and the heat. I don't think I would have survived—"

"It really wasn't that bad, Mom," I interrupted. "In fact, I got used to a lot of things. It's amazing to find out what you don't really need in life."

"I know what I really need," she said very firmly. "I need a hot shower every morning and time to put on my makeup and do my hair and plenty of clean clothes. I would never have survived," she repeated.

"Well, I survived and pretty well, too," I said.

"I don't know how you did it. I'm just glad I was on a nice luxurious ship with Felix to carry my bags whenever we went shopping in a port."

As Mom talked, I began to feel absolutely

dreadful. Had I really sounded like her just a few weeks before? I blushed now as I remembered myself commanding Bruce to load my baggage. Would I become like Mom again if I went back to live with her? But how could I tell her I didn't want to go back to Westchester without hurting her feelings? Then I got a great idea. "You're absolutely right, Mom," I said. "And I just can't wait until we move to New York City. After all this primitive living, I'm really ready for some civilization, a few fancy, expensive restaurants, some of those wild, all-night dance clubs. Just wait until I hit the Fifth Avenue stores. I'm going to get a whole new wardrobe." I went on and on.

Slowly I felt my mother getting less and less enthusiastic about bringing me to New York. "Now don't go overboard, dear. You're only sixteen."

"Oh, but I'll lead a whole new sophisticated life," I said.

"Well, um, we haven't even found a new apartment yet. You know the one Felix has is too small for the three of us. It's hard to find a place in the city. It may take a long time."

"You're right, Mom," I agreed, "and I wouldn't want to hold up any of your plans. So, why don't you let me stay with Dad in California?

When you do find an apartment, then I'll come home."

"Well—" my mother hesitated, "I'll have to think it over." But I knew by the way she said it that the answer would be yes. Anything to keep me from that sophisticated New York life I'd described to her. Anything, that is, except mess up her plans with Felix. And I also knew that once she got comfortable in Felix's apartment, it would be easy to convince her to let me stay in California. I got off the phone with Mom knowing I'd gotten what I wanted. I went outside to find Bruce and tell him I'd solved at least one of my problems.

"So there you are," Bruce called, running up the slope toward me. He had been swimming in the sea, and water still dripped from his hair and sparkled on his eyelashes. "You should have come. It was terrific."

"I called my mother in Westchester," I said.

"Did you manage to sort things out?" he asked, running a towel through his wet hair.

"It's not definite," I said, "but I got the impression Mom wouldn't be heartbroken if I didn't live with her."

"So why didn't you come right out and tell her you want to stay in California?"

"For the same reason that you won't come right out and tell your father you don't want to go into his business. She'd be hurt if I said I didn't want her anymore."

"Hey, you know, that's not such a bad idea!" he said smiling mysteriously at me. "I just might try it." Bruce gave me a quick kiss and dashed off. I went into the house to find my father.

I found him in the library, reading about one of the earliest outback expeditions. "Dad, I talked to Mom on the phone just now. She needs a little time to get things ready in the city. She wants me to stay with you a few more weeks."

"I gather your mother thinks the apartment in New York will be too small for three people," my father said dryly.

"Yes, so I won't be flying back to Westchester immediately."

"Are you upset about that?" he asked.

"I couldn't have gone back there," I said. "I'd have had to get out of it somehow."

"I see," he said. There was a pause.

"So it looks like you're stuck with me for a while longer," I said uneasily. "Is that OK with you? I mean, I've probably caused you enough trouble already."

"Honey," he said quietly, "that's the best news I've had all year."

I looked up at his face, and there was a little tear on his cheek. "Oh, Dad," I said and flung myself into his arms.

The awful day had finally come—the day that I'd be flying back to America. Bruce had been very quiet for the last couple of days, but that day, our last day together, he seemed happy again. Every time I looked at him, there was a little secret smile on his lips.

"You're looking very pleased with yourself," I commented as we walked hand in hand down the beach. "I'm beginning to think you'll be glad to get rid of me."

He looked at me and grinned. "Come on, let's go for a swim," he said, suddenly dragging me toward the water.

"But, Bruce, wait a minute, I haven't even taken off my shorts," I protested as the waves broke over us. Then he was holding me in his strong arms, kissing me as the waves tumbled us into the shore. "You'd make a great lifeguard," I said, panting as both the waves and Bruce released me. "If you gave mouth-to-mouth resuscitation like that, you'd have the girls all lining up to drown."

"Not me," he said. "I'm strictly a private lifeguard for only one person. The others will all just have to drown."

Bruce sat down on the sand and pulled me down next to him.

"But you won't even see that one person after tomorrow," I said in a small voice.

"I might just come and visit from time to time—if you want me to, that is."

"All the way from Australia? You're crazy," I said.

"No, not from Australia, from UCLA."

"UCLA?" I said barely whispering. "You mean in Los Angeles?"

"I don't think there's one anyplace else," he said.

"You mean that's the college you've applied to?" I yelled. "Why didn't you tell me before?"

He was laughing, those wonderful blue eyes sparkling like the ocean before us. "I didn't want to say anything until I knew my dad would really let me go," he said. "No sense in getting our hopes up for nothing."

"So, you actually *will* be able to come and visit all the time!" I cried, wrapping my arms around his neck.

"Get one thing straight, I'll be studying hard," he said in a teasing voice, "so don't expect me to come running to visit you every evening. I've got to get great grades and a degree in environmental science to prove to my dad that college isn't a waste of time."

"How on earth did you get him to agree to let you go?" I asked. "Especially all the way in Los Angeles?"

"I sort of tricked him into it," Bruce said. "Your dad helped, too, by explaining to him that the program at UCLA is exceptional."

"Bruce, that's fantastic! But what do you mean, you tricked him into it?" I asked.

"Pretty much the way you got your mother to let you stay in California. I suddenly decided to become very keen on working with my old man, and I came up with all kinds of suggestions for making everything run better. I thought of some really wacky ones. So Dad decided to let me go to college first and get rid of all my bright ideas there."

"I can't believe it," I said. "And I thought I'd never see you again."

"I told you things have a way of working themselves out," he said. "Now don't waste precious time by talking!" He drew me close, and his mouth met mine.

It was a kiss I knew I'd remember for the rest of my life, even though I was looking forward to many sequels when he arrived in L.A. "That was what I call a perfect ending," I said, gazing into his eyes.

NOW IS THE TIME TO START A NEW ROMANCE . . . AND

IS THE ROMANCE SERIES TO GET YOU STARTED!

You'll find all the romance, adventure, action and excitement you dream about— in books that make all those dreams come true right before you. Books like

☐ **P.S. I LOVE YOU #1 by Barbara Conklin** (14019-1 • $1.95)
Nothing makes a summer special like falling in love. With Paul, Palm Springs becomes the most romantic place on earth. But Paul is seriously ill. Will Mariah lose Paul just when she's found her first love?

☐ **LITTLE SISTER #5 by Yvonne Greene** (24319-5 • $2.25)
Cindy feels she's going to play second fiddle to Christine all her life. Then she meets Ron, and this time *she's* #1. But when her older sister steps in again, it seems like Cindy will lose Ron—unless she can prove she's not second best after all.

☐ **CALIFORNIA GIRL #6 by Janet Quin-Harkin**
(22995-8 • $1.95)
Jennie was determined to be an Olympic competitor. Then she falls for Mark, an ex-football star with a serious leg injury. Secretly, Jenny enters Mark in a drawing contest, and he's an overnight success—but he may leave Jenny behind. Jenny's so confused she can't concentrate on her swimming. Will she lose her love and a chance at her Olympic dream?

☐ **GREEN EYES #7 by Suzanne Rand** (24321-7 • $2.25)
Julie's had a crush on Dan ever since sophomore year. Now she finally has him all to herself. But when Dan even *talks* to another girl, Julie becomes insanely jealous. Will Julie's crazy jealousy destroy the love she waited so long to find?

☐ **HOW DO YOU SAY GOODBYE #16 by Margaret Burman** (22517-0 • $1.95)
Lisa really likes Alex, but she's afraid to hurt Lawrence. So she goes steady with both of them and lives a double life of lies and confusion—until the night when her lies go too far.

☐ **FORBIDDEN LOVE #35 by Marian Woodruff** (23338-6 • $1.95)
When Patti backs into Tim's car in the school parking lot, it turns out to be the beginning of a wonderful relationship. But their parents start arguing about the accident, and Patti and Tim are forbidden to see each other. Why won't their parents just listen?

There are over 60 Sweet Dreams books in all—and two new ones are published every month! All are available at your local bookstore (or use this handy coupon to order the titles listed above).

Coming Soon . . .

Watch for the
SWEET VALLEY HIGH/SOAP OPERA
CELEBRATION CONTEST

Here's your chance to win an exciting all-expense-paid trip to New York City for three.

If you're one of the lucky winners . . .*

> You'll take in the fabulous sights of New York City, see a Broadway show and visit a top beauty salon for a complete makeover!

> You'll visit the set of ABC-TV's popular daytime drama, *All My Children*, and watch as your favorite soap stars rehearse another exciting episode!

> You'll meet the creator of Sweet Valley High, Francine Pascal, in the elegant surroundings of one of the finest restaurants in New York!

Watch for complete contest details at your local bookseller starting August, 1984!

*There will be two winners—one from the United States and one from Canada. The contest will apply only to Canada, the continental U.S., Alaska and Hawaii.

Be sure to watch *All My Children* weekdays on ABC-TV (check local listings).

☐	23969-4	**DOUBLE LOVE #1** Francine Pascal	**$2.25**
☐	23971	**SECRETS #2** Francine Pascal	**$2.25**
☐	23972	**PLAYING WITH FIRE #3** Francine Pascal	**$2.25**
☐	23730	**POWER PLAY #4** Francine Pascal	**$2.25**
☐	23943	**ALL NIGHT LONG #5** Francine Pascal	**$2.25**
☐	23938	**DANGEROUS LOVE #6** Francine Pascal	**$2.25**
☐	24001	**DEAR SISTER #7** Francine Pascal	**$2.25**
☐	24045	**HEARTBREAKER #8** Francine Pascal	**$2.25**
☐	24131	**LOVE ON THE RUN #9** Francine Pascal	**$2.25**
☐	24182	**WRONG KIND OF GIRL #10** Francine Pascal	**$2.25**
☐	24252	**TOO GOOD TO BE TRUE #11** Francine Pascal	**$2.25**

Prices and availability subject to change without notice.

Buy them at your local bookstore or use this handy coupon for ordering:

SPECIAL
MONEY SAVING
OFFER

Now you can have an up to date listing of Bantam's hundreds of titles plus take advantage of our unique and exciting bonus book offer. A special offer which gives you the opportunity to purchase a Bantam book for only 50¢. Here's how!

By ordering any five books at the regular price per order, you can also choose any other single book listed (up to a $4.95 value) for just 50¢. Some restrictions do apply, but for further details why not send for Bantam's listing of titles today!

Just send us your name and address plus 50¢ to defray the postage and handling costs.